Beyond Extinction

Judgment In Time Series Book V

BEYOND EXTINCTION

New People Publishing

Follow us on Facebook and Twitter to keep up with
Judgment In Time conversations and updates

 Facebook: www.facebook.com \ JITSeries
Twitter: @JITSeries

Available in Hardcover, Paperback, and
eBook as ePub, Kindle, and Nook

Fiction: Action and Adventure, Time Travel, Science Fiction, Supernatural, Romance, Mystery, Thriller

Judgment In Time Series

Book I: Judgment In Time
Book II: Imagine A New World
Book III: Another Fine Mess
Book IV: Another Side of Armageddon
Book V: Beyond Extinction
Book VI: Judgment of the Gods

New People Publishing
www.NewPeoplePublishing.com

Editor: Robert Allen Fisher
Cover Art and Full Page Illustrations: Jennifer Cole
Production Design and Illustrations: Tom Hultgren

ISBN-13: 978-0-9990580-6-0
Advance Edition: Trade Paperback

Printed in the United States of America by:
Lightning Source

10 9 8 7 6 5 4 3 2 1

About the Author

Kevin Klesert, a successful independent businessman, has experienced firsthand how small businesses all over the country carried a disproportionate amount of the burden to meet their legal obligations. The steady erosion of Main Street USA under mountains of onerous regulations, licenses, taxes, and fees from Federal, State, and Local Governments have all but destroyed their ability to succeed and turn a reasonable profit.

His intense study of historical trends brought to him the correlation between the downfall of dominant societies of the past and the current struggle to maintain the most noble and ambitious political experiment in human history, the United States of America. He discovered the seeds of ruin were planted within the very generation that launched the United States to world preeminence.

Kevin Klesert's desire to shed light on this dire situation through the means of a thrilling adventure has produced a story worthy of the fight against these negative forces. The ideas for the Judgment In Time Series percolated in his adventurous imagination while he raised his four children and ran an award-winning design and construction company. A 3rd generation native of Southern California, Kevin Klesert imbues his writing with his passion for history, adventure, and fantasy.

Table of Contents

Characters

Human Characters

Rear Admiral UH Retired Sean Phillips – Former Commanding Officer, Enterprise Task Force, now married to Admiral Alicia Calhoun

Captain Anthony Knox – Former Chief of Staff to Admiral Sean Phillips, now married to Captain Renée Aslan

Rear Admiral UH Retired Alicia Calhoun – Former Secretary of Defense, now married to Admiral Sean Phillips

Captain Renée Aslan – Former Naval Attaché to Alicia Calhoun, now married to Captain Anthony Knox

Dr. Rebecca Cutler Eddington, PhD – Former Comstock Technologies Lead Specter Engineer, married to Captain Carl Eddington

Captain Daniel Osaka – Former Commanding Officer, USS Enterprise

Commander Michael *Thorny* Thornton – Task Force SEAL Commander

Phoenix – Black Hat Hacker, married to Sean Anthony Eddington

Adonis – Black Hat Hacker

Lydia Eddington – Daughter of Sean Anthony and Phoenix

Supernatural Characters

Captain Carl Eddington – Darius in Human Form, married to Rebecca

Darius – Durius' Ex, Aaron's Father, Sean Anthony's Father

Durius – Darius' Ex, Aaron's Mother

Jesus – Cromulus in Human Form

Cosmo – Advanced Supernatural Entity

Sean Anthony Eddington – Advanced Entity, Son of Carl and Rebecca

Aaron Fletcher – Advanced Entity, Son of Darius [Carl] and Durius

Advanced Entity Impersonating Benjamin Franklin

Advanced Entity Impersonating Various David Bowie Personas

Characters Continued

Supernatural Imprinter Characters, Attributes, & Lineage

Darius [Carl], Male, Contributed Attribute – Creativity
    Lineage – Sean Phillips

Durius, Female – Sister to Kalius, Contributed Attribute – Honor
    Lineage – Anthony Knox, Commander *Thorny* Thornton

Cromulus [Jesus], Male, Contributed Attribute – Purity
    – Daniel Osaka

Kalius, Female – Sister to Durius, Contributed Attribute – Wisdom
    Lineage – Renée Aslan

Surius, Male, Contributed Attribute – Empathy
    Lineage – Alicia Calhoun, Lydia Eddington

Perculus, Female, Contributed Attribute – Intellect
    Lineage – Rebecca and Phoenix Eddington, Adonis

Part I
Where Are We Now?

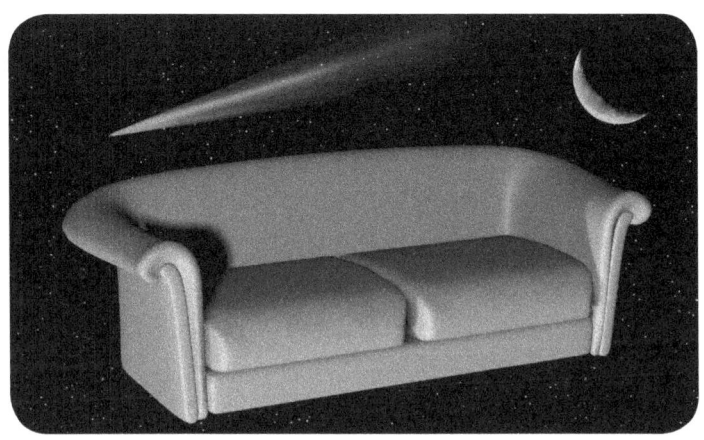

A contented Benjamin Franklin swayed to the music as he listened to David Bowie perform.

"Pack a packhorse and rest up here
On Black Country Rock
You never know what you will find there
On Black Country Rock."

As the last verse ended, the musicians who backed Bowie began to fade with the music, leaving the two icons alone in the house.

After Bowie put his guitar down, a lit cigarette appeared between the fingers of his right hand, from which he then took a deep drag. "I must say I never saw this coming. I was bloody sure she would crack after the first one hundred years, especially leaving her alone the way you did. I should write a song about it. How does the title *Regeneration By God* sound?"

Franklin reacted to the idea by waving his handkerchief in the air as if to remove a foul stench. "For someone who considers himself to be an artist, you can sure come up with some juvenile banalities. How about instead you come up with a spectacular ending to this story?"

"Since when is the ending ever pivotal to the story?" Three simple pages appeared on the table in front of the couch. Bowie picked one up and read from it. "Man or woman conquers a list of impossible tasks, and hugs the grateful sobbing husband, wife, BFF, or child."

Bowie crumpled the page, tossed it over his shoulder, and picked up the next one. "Boy hates girl or guy, becomes BFF, loses BFF, falls in love, breaks up, and the shock of shocks ending, ends up in the wedding chapel, fade out, roll credits." Paper crumbled, tossed.

"And last of all, my least favorite, two buddies, either men or women, share blissful BFF relationship, one is threatened, other fights either cops, criminals, or aliens to save BFF, walk off while drinking a cold one after murdering everything in sight."

Paper crumbled, this time tossed in Franklin's face. "The one thing you can most assuredly count on from these humans is to repeat the same tired stories ad nauseam. From a purely artistic perspective, the species haven't had an original thought since Homer wrote the Iliad and the Odyssey."

Franklin didn't agree. "There is a kernel of truth in what you say, but it does not account for the thousands of interpretations of these original ideas that allow the masses to connect with them. Provided Sean and Alicia save the day, it will be the strengths and weaknesses of each person that creates something new out of the old story."

Bowie feigned a yawn while stretching his arms. "Seen it all before. All story telling is subjective to who wrote it. When the reader who interprets the story thinks they understand the message, they are full of shit. That is, unless they have dwelled in the creator's deepest thoughts like Shakespeare or Mel Brooks."

Familiar with this game, Franklin responded, "Way too simplistic my good friend. Without the written word or a beautiful piece of art, there is nothing left of the human soul but brutality."

Happy to continue the debate, Bowie upped his energy with

a quick bump. "The scourge of true artistry came the day the Sumerians thought it would be a good idea to memorialize their existence by carving it into some wet clay. Since then, every egotist has felt compelled to follow suit. These days, to find a true nugget of originality one must first dive into an ocean of mediocrity to discover a single pearl of beauty."

Though Franklin agreed with much of what Bowie said regarding the nature of what passed for centuries of their art, he felt compelled to continue. "Andy Warhol, really? It took one thousand years of darkness before the Renaissance brought color back into the world of man, and that led directly to the Reformation and the Age of Reason. So who is to say these creatures don't have another Renaissance in them?"

Bowie laughed. "Great, you are arguing that a few bright ideas every half a millennium is worth waiting for? Especially while they spend every waking hour improving how they can destroy one another, and by the way massacring every other living creature on the planet as they go about it. Besides, you know as well as I do these bursts of creativity are always a direct result of Darius' intervention."

"Does this include how you interpret all of David Bowie's personas?" Franklin inquired.

"Yes I do. Every piece of his performance art was merely bits and pieces of other artists he used to create characters that are out of step with the times he represents. His shtick is a direct descendant from the burlesque of 1930s Paris. What goes around always comes around because there is a written history to remind us. It is only original if there isn't a place to find out it already existed, ergo lose the history so no one knows better."

Satisfied with his logic, Bowie ended with a flourish. "That over the last ten thousand years, Darius buried ten different human civilizations, each more advanced than the one we are currently playing in, validates my argument."

Franklin applauded Bowie's conviction by clapping his hands. "I especially love it when you argue against your own hubris."

"You may enjoy that we became involved in this drudgery Franklin, but I was perfectly satisfied with the life I had before Darius pushed us into saving the humans. As much as I enjoy experiencing these strange creature's idiosyncrasies, I would rather head back if it is all the same to you."

Franklin snorted his disapproval. "Taking your toys and going home because we are not central to what needs to happen right now so becomes you. For once in your impetuous life, why not sit back and stick around to watch how they react to what happened to their world. Regardless of how limited you believe their chances of survival are it still might be entertaining to watch them go down fighting. Contrary to your protestations, the diva in you wouldn't have it any other way."

Without waiting for a response, Franklin reached down, picked up the remote from the table, and turned the monitor on. The screen lit up to display an aerial view looking down on a fleet of warships at anchor. Instead of the usual blue waters one associates with the ocean, a constantly shifting sea of colors surrounded the ships. Only the outline of the bay revealed the location to be the Chesapeake Bay, as all traces of the modern cities that grew up around it had disappeared.

A bottle of wine and a plate of cheeses appeared for Franklin, and a bowl of popcorn, cocaine grinder, bong, and enough junk food to last a week appeared for Bowie as he took a seat on the couch.

With a shake of his head in disgust, Bowie gave in to the inevitable. "Fantastic. So we are now relegated to watching a soap opera?"

He then fished from his pockets a vial of coke and a bag of weed that he offered to Franklin.

Instead, Franklin reached for the bottle of wine. "Better the poison I know. Are you up for a quick recap before moving forward?"

"Only the highlights, please. You know how I detest looking back."

Franklin hit rewind and stopped when the scene shifted to UFOs menacing Washington D.C. Seconds later the entire district, along with the surrounding environs began to deconstruct in a visual display rivaling anything Michael Bay could cook up.

The scene then shifted to a closeup of the Capitol Building and the horrified looks of the citizens who crowded the steps. Above their heads, they watched in stunned silence as the statue of Lady Liberty that topped the dome rapidly disintegrated; their silence shattered by screams of terror as the entire dome followed suit. Mass panic erupted when it became clear that within seconds the disruption of the rest of the sprawling monument would include them.

By the time the last of the edifice disappeared, momentum, along with the deconstructed mass of the surrounding buildings coming together, swept like a tidal wave over the remaining survivors, who could only stand in frozen horror as they too broke apart into trillions of atoms.

Bowie was not impressed. "Twenty-seven thousand years of planetary history unzipped in seconds. Those Greys should learn how to soak up the drama of the moment. Absolutely no sense of showmanship, if you ask me."

Franklin agreed. "I'm surprised Aaron missed the chance to demand that as part of the deal. Considering how badly he got his ass handed to him, one would think slow motion with multiple cut away shots of babies ripping apart would have been more his style."

Franklin poured a glass from the wine bottle and took a moment to savor its clarity before he continued. "I must admit though, his turning to the Greys didn't surprise me. He always struck me as the spoiled child who takes his ball and goes home when he doesn't get his way. On the bright side, it is a sheer joy to witness the product of unlimited entitlement receiving his comeuppance for a change. Who knows, maybe he can learn something from the experience?"

Bowie rolled his eyes in disbelief. "You say that as if he is the one we should be worried about." The tone in Bowie's voice betrayed his underlying fear. "You know all this means is the prologue has ended, and the real battle begins." He leaned down with a gold tube in his nose and vacuumed up three fat lines. "Next time it will not be only the denizens of that reality she deconstructs."

Franklin laughed at his friend's fear of Durius. "You do know you can say her name without the gates of Hell opening up and swallowing us, don't you. Durius, Durius, Durius." Franklin scanned the room in a circle and raised his hands in the air in mock surrender. "We have sinned oh mighty Goddess Durius. Come down from on high and smite those whom you deem unworthy."

"You do realize it is I that is supposed to be the out of control crazy artist type while you charm with wistful intellect. Why would you wish to bollocks everything up by tempting the fates now?"

Franklin laughed at Bowie's sudden caution. "This coming from the person who stuck his tongue in a certain potentate's ear, at least I think it was its ear. Anyway, because of that little lack of decorum, we will never enjoy such complex cuisine again, let alone the company of some of the most dexterous creatures in this sector of the galaxy."

Franklin refilled his wine glass while he waited for Bowie's rebuttal. When it didn't arrive, he moved on. "That's enough speculation about Aaron and the dangers of Durius. I am much more curious about how Anthony and Renée are adjusting." Franklin switched channels until he found them. "There they all are. Let's start from here."

After brunch ended, the four walked over to an open-top vehicle that looked like a scaled down Austin Martin. Tony unplugged it, and both he and Renée got in. "According to the Gospel of Franklin, we have another year until something happens."

"Let's enjoy the peace and quiet for as long as it lasts. Besides, only the four of us know about the 100-year mark," Sean stated as he and Alicia waved goodbye.

"Rodger that boss." With a final wave, Tony hit the pedal and drove off. A half hour later they were back at the home Franklin installed him in all those decades ago. He kept it, not because of Franklin, but because this is where Renée had returned to him from the dead. He parked the car and they headed to the door. Upon entering, they experienced their first shock in years. In the living room, Franklin and Bowie stood smiling. Seated on the couch, Sean and Alicia looked extremely unhappy.

"Did you miss us?' Bowie was back in Ziggy mode, while Franklin maintained his customary buttoned up brown colonial suit.

"This can't be good. What now, is there a Zargon space fleet entering Earth orbit and you need us to tickle their feet into defeat." Tony walked by them and reached for the bottle of rum from his still.

"Zargon fleet, tickle, that is hilarious. I have so missed your rapier wit, Anthony." A bottle of wine appeared next to the rum. "You know I prefer wine. Would you mind pouring?"

"Since when don't you conjure up your own glass, and where's your coke and weed? Isn't that a part of your Ziggy persona?"

Bowie ignored Tony's sarcasm. "I am dressed to honor my first appearance with this lovely couple." He turned his gaze toward Sean and Alicia. "That and to compliment the four of you again for achieving such grand results. Would you mind pouring me one while you are at it, but could you make mine rum?"

Reluctantly Tony complied, and after everyone had a drink, he and Renée sat down next to each other and waited to hear how their lives were going to change again.

"You leave us here for a century…" Sean paused to gather his thoughts. After all, he had a lot of time to think about this moment. "That's right; believe it or not we have been here for one hundred years, and after all that time, you still haven't given us a clue why or what this is all about. Is that why you are here now, to finally expose your dirty little secrets?" Sean wasn't much for delaying the inevitable.

"What no foreplay?"

Franklin motioned for Bowie to stop and then continued, totally ignoring Sean's question. "To put it simply, you are finished, and it is time to go home."

Thinking that his time with Renée was about to end, Tony frantically asked, "Wait, what about the year we have left?"

Franklin's news caused Alicia to ignore both Tony and Sean's questions. "What do you mean go home? If you refer to the place we spent less than a third of our lives, I don't believe any of us will call that home anymore."

Then Renée voiced a concern unique to her. "My understanding was if Tony left, I would cease to exist. Is that still true?"

Franklin tilted his head down, so his eyes were above his bifocals. "My dear, by my count there are hundreds of your offspring roaming throughout the Americas. You are everywhere, and besides, I said you couldn't go, not that you would not exist."

Tony stood up so fast his drink spilled. "What the hell does that mean? If you think I am going anywhere without her, you're crazy."

Franklin dispensed with the posturing and revealed a look of genuine sadness. "For reasons that may or may not become clear to you, I can say I regret that this must be."

Franklin then leaned in close so only Tony and Renée could hear what he said. "Somewhere in the back of both of your minds, you knew this day would come. Well, that day is today. If there is to be any chance for the world that you all so brilliantly reformed to survive, Tony must leave it."

Sean could tell from whatever Franklin had said that Tony was about to explode. "You know, for most of our time here, Tony has conjectured that our being here has absolutely no other purpose than to entertain some higher civilization. I think I am starting to come around to such an insane idea. What about you, Alicia, do you think they are capable of yanking our chains like that?"

Alicia had her concerns. "So what is going to become of this world if we are not here to continue to safeguard it from reverting to its old habits? Then there is that tiny little problem of after a century of living here, all of those families in this reality being torn apart, and our sailors returning to loved ones who haven't had time to miss them. Sounds like chaos on a monumental scale to me."

"That's up to Renée." Once again, Franklin failed to address their concerns.

As the room filled with green mist, they all knew it would remain that way.

The last shared memory Sean, Alicia, Tony, and Renée had together was of Tony and Renée's frenzied attempt to embrace each other.

In Guantanamo Bay and everywhere else the Enterprise Task Force ships, aircraft, equipment, and personnel existed, the green mist made them all disappear. All that remained in the 1492 reality of what came from the 2018 reality was a shocked Renée. "Son of a bitch!"

Renée collapsed on the living room couch crying, all alone in the house Franklin had built for Tony in Cuba. That is until a cheery voice called to her from the kitchen. "Do you prefer Scotch or Jack Daniels?"

Recognizing Franklin's voice, she called back, "Scotch," as she pulled herself together and headed for the kitchen.

"Where did you send my friends and my husband, and why am I the only one still here?" Renée gruffly demanded, knowing she would not like the answer.

Franklin put one hand on her shoulder while he handed her the tumbler of Scotch with the other. "Well child, we need someone here to make sure this planet survives in this reality, and I am sorry to inform you that you were the only viable option."

———✦———

Moments after leaving Cuba in the green mist, Sean, Alicia, and Tony were once again in the Admirals Ready Room on the Enterprise with klaxons ringing General Quarters. When Tony noticed is wife Renée was not with them, he threw the half-filled glass that was still in his hand against the bulkhead.

Unfortunately for Tony, this wasn't the first time he lost track of Renée. She had died from gunshots she received in 1942 at the hands of Southern racists in front of the US Capitol. Shortly thereafter, Sean, Alicia, and four of the Enterprise Task Force ships disappeared leaving him alone. He spent the next nine years in the 1942 reality disillusioned and disengaged.

While on the bridge of the USS Missouri in 1951, the green mist transported him to the wilderness of the late 15th Century Cuba. With a little help from a powerful entity in the form of Benjamin Franklin, he spent spend the next two years helping the Taíno prepare for the arrival of Christopher Columbus.

Once Tony and the Taíno destroyed the Niña, Pinta, Santa Maria, and all their crews while still at sea, as promised, Benjamin Franklin miraculously resurrected Renée. Only then did Tony begin to return to his former self.

Risking both life and limb, Alicia put her hand on his shoulder. "Easy there tiger. Why don't you take a step back until we figure out what's going on?"

Fortunately, this was enough to redirect his rage. "Fine! Let's go figure it out." Tony didn't wait for a reply as he stormed out of the room, with Sean following right behind.

"I'll stay here to find out if anyone is at their post." Alicia picked up the phone to call the CIC; however, since it had not been operational for decades, decided instead to call the bridge. To her surprise, Captain Daniel Osaka's voice answered.

"You better get topside." From the tone of his voice, something had seriously freaked him out. "You are not going to believe the chaos we are in the middle of."

First Tony, now the usually unflappable Osaka sounded as though he had lost it. "Captain please calm down and tell me exactly why we are at General Quarters on a ship that hasn't been crewed for the last fifty years?"

"We're at General Quarters because there is absolutely nothing outside to give us a single reference point to determine if this ship is sitting in a body of water, or on a different planet."

Though Alicia could tell he was attempting to sound calm, none of what he was saying made any sense. "I'll be right there." Once she entered the corridor, she realized there wasn't anyone else around, and decided to head to the flight deck instead. "If something weird is going on, no better place to take a look," she said to herself.

When Alicia stepped through the hatch that led to the flight deck, she could see Sean and Tony standing near the starboard edge. As she walked toward them, she understood why Osaka sounded so stressed out. Instead of the ocean, the ship floated amid multi-colored waves that moved in erratic patterns. "Where did they send us this time?"

Sean turned around at the sound of her voice. "We need to get our bearings."

Alicia grabbed Sean's hand, and with the other pointed toward the bow of the ship. "There appears to be a rise in elevation over there about half a mile out."

Sean looked where Alicia directed and began to make out other features as they rose above the swirling chaos. "That's Norfolk, I think. At least what used to be Norfolk."

Tony looked at his friend. "Did I miss something and we traveled to another planet where we named chaos Norfolk?"

They remained silent for a moment, mesmerized by the craziness of their new environment, until Alicia broke the spell. "Wherever Renée is, it can't be as weird as this."

Suddenly alone on the flight deck, Tony was about to scream out every profanity known to the sailor's dictionary when he too began to disappear. In disgust, he threw his hands up in the air, the middle finger extended on both. "Franklin!"

Admiral Sean Phillips had a bit of a problem, and because this problem happened to be the extra consciousness that occupied his, he found it difficult to digest his new environment.

His wife, Admiral Alicia Calhoun shared his confusion. "Imagine how I feel, honey."

They found Sean's body seated on an overstuffed couch in a typically upscale suburban home neither recognized. Across from Sean sat one of Sean's former commanders, though a much older version of the man. "It's been a long time Commander Eddington. Would I be out of line if I were to understand that you have had a rather large hand in all of this?"

Instead of giving Sean an answer Carl offered, "I do believe you have had the pleasure of meeting our son."

Seated next to Sean was Carl and Dr. Rebecca Cutler's son Sean Anthony Eddington, the young man who long ago in that Spanish dungeon had saved Sean and Alicia from Carl's other son, Aaron Fletcher.

Sean chose to let Alicia take over the conversation. "It has been a long time Sean Anthony. Where's your mother?" Alicia attempted to shake his hand, but she could not command Sean's body to react.

"At the moment she is filling your companions in about their current situation. It is a pleasure to see you still safe and sound, and to thank you for taking such good care of my mother."

Alicia shook her head in the negative. "If not for your mother there is no doubt any of us would still be alive., It has been too long since we had the pleasure of her company, those days being so long ago."

Though Sean agreed with Alicia, that he shared her mind in his body made for an impossible situation. That he could feel Alicia's thoughts forming before she spoke them began to unhinge him. "As much as I have made a point to know everything about you, sweetheart, this is all a little too much."

All too much, when he considered how little he understood about Alicia's actual thought processes. Thoughts such as the regrets she still held about never raising a family, while at the same time greeting Sean Anthony.

Surprisingly to Alicia, this ultimate invasion of her privacy didn't bother her as much as she would have thought. Besides, it worked both ways. "That's okay; who knew under that exterior of restraint of yours beat the heart of a hopeless romantic. I now know why you and Tony get along so well."

Much to his discomfort, Sean could tell Alicia wanted to dig deeper into his thoughts, feelings, and memories. To further his chagrin, she enjoyed his discomfort more than he would like. "Who knew you could be so demanding. I thought what you loved about me is my ability to control my emotions under stress. Just because I am in love with the idea of a world that never existed, doesn't mean I don't see the one we live in for what it is."

Alicia could not resist one last dig. "Dragons, fair maidens, and villains, oh my."

"You might want to slow down girl. I can see buried under all of your heterosexual conformity some regret that you never experimented. You still paint a rather interesting picture of that redhead roomie of yours who made the failed attempt."

Carl and Sean Anthony watched with amusement as Sean's face flushed red. Carl sat patiently through their internal exchange, but the minute the conversation played out, he took pity on Sean. As Sean Anthony moved over to the chair next to him, Carl leaned forward and tapped Sean on the forehead. Alicia instantly appeared on the couch next to her husband.

Wasting no time to regain his equilibrium, Sean hit the ground running. He directed his confusion about their current situation directly at Carl. "Was that necessary? Where are we and what happened to my people?"

Carl responded in a manner that would have made even the most evolved feminist proud. "I thought it would be a wonderful opportunity for you to see further into your soul mate before what comes next. I have ensured that your ships and crew are safe for now, which is more than I can say about many others."

Though spoken in a fatherly manner, Carl's response did nothing to reassure either Sean or Alicia. "When you say safe for now, safe from what?" Sean asked. "And what do you mean by *many others*?"

Alicia chimed in. "Is Tony still with them, and are they still in the 16th Century?"

"Let's say that all of your paths are diverging for now and leave it at that." Then Carl's inflections portended an ominous future. "The others are unimportant for what lies ahead for you two." Carl didn't see any point in bringing up that their entire 2018 home reality had turned into a deconstructed mass.

This attitude set Sean off. He launched off the couch and began to pace the room. "So for over the decade you served under me, you not only masqueraded as a naval officer, but also pretended to be a human being. So I have to ask, is this all a game to you? And is there a whole race of others such as you?"

Carl's response wasn't what either Sean or Alicia expected. "First off, I certainly did not pretend to be anything. Carl Eddington is as real as anyone in this room is. Second, not to make you feel inferior, but that is exactly how we viewed your planet and everything on it for millions of your years. You and everything you know to be true are merely figments of my imagination, and that is the crux of the crisis that led us to where we are today."

Alicia didn't like where this was headed. "So now you are God, and we are simply your children who are being severely punished for our wicked ways?"

"Do you think you should be disciplined? Without a doubt, the human race is one of the most self-absorbed species in the entire galaxy. If not for my love for Rebecca, I probably would have let humanity end without a second thought."

Sean Anthony thought now would be a good time to intercede. "What Dad is trying to say is he is all in and doing everything within his power to save us from those who helped create the savage reality your world has experienced for most of its existence. His goal is to rebuild it and humanity with those as like-minded as you. It is also why you experienced the shared consciousness. He wanted to avoid unnecessary drama between you two."

This gave both Sean and Alicia something to chew on for a minute, before Alicia reacted first. "That must mean that you and Rebecca go back much further than one typical human lifespan."

Carl needed to avoid going too far down the rabbit hole, but he knew at this moment he needed to be honest with them. "Where do you think the Greeks found the material to create their Gods? In those days I enjoyed the worship more than I would care to admit.

"Through her eyes, I witnessed something unique and different from everything that came before. My hubris kept me from seeing what was in front of me all along. Just because I create it, doesn't mean it is any longer mine. At the time of this epiphany, I lived in Italy as Giacomo Da Lentini, who as I am sure you are unaware, created the sonnet. I am also responsible for most of all early written romance, most of which I learned from watching you two. Anyway, because I…"

Alicia interrupted. "Go back to the part about watching us."

Carl smiled and waved it off. "We will save that one for later.

Now, as I was saying, because of my love for a human, the one you would refer to as my mate took exception to my dalliance. Unfortunately, as you can imagine, this created its own set of problems, which to be quite honest are also not worth dwelling on. However, most of the chaos, violence, and corruption most humans blame themselves for are not entirely their fault. Because this has inexcusably gone on far too long, we are in the middle of reversing it, and that is why you are here alone with us."

Sean felt himself losing his emotional footing upon hearing how little he or any other human controlled their destiny or even their thoughts. "Of all of those you have moved through time and space with, why us? Now might be the time to throw us a bone. Hell, if only Rebecca matters, why not create the perfect world for her and jettison of the rest of the riff raff."

Sean Anthony empathized with his turmoil. "Contrary to Dad's apparent lack of sensitivity, he is using every trick at his command to bring the best of humanity to the forefront. To answer your question regarding why you; it is because you possess the qualities he has spent thousands of years working to bring to all of humanity. Now we will discover if it is all for naught."

"None of that does anything to explain why you felt it necessary to send an entire naval task force along for the ride." Alicia added to the pressure Sean had attempted to exert on Carl and Sean Anthony. "Exactly how many realities are there, and why did the Nazi carrier have Sean's name on the stern?"

Sean thought back to that horrible day when he was responsible for the loss of thousands of lives when he ordered the destruction of the Nazi carrier task force.

Carl gave Alicia's questions a moment of thought before he answered. "How many alternative realities exist? As many as your imagination can dream up." As Carl spoke, the room faded away, replaced by a Roman spa whose heated waters they now sat naked in, surrounded by many strangers. "Some people experience what you refer to as Déjà vu, which, contrary to expert opinion, is actually a means by which your subconscious can travel to places such as this."

The spa faded out and they sat facing a window with an incredible view of deep space. Carl directed them to turn around where they discovered what appeared to be a massive multistoried mall. "And this is what could be your future. The idea of thousands of human pioneers traveling the cosmos, spreading humanity to any uninhabited world hospitable enough to support it.

"If we succeed, you will join millions of other life forms in a universe you cannot yet comprehend." As Carl finished, they sat once again in the living room where they began.

Though still overwhelmed by the experience, Sean responded. "I must admit I have never met anyone so adept at diverting attention away from the questions asked as you. In no world I can think of have I dreamed of me as a Nazi, reformed or not."

Sean Anthony jumped back in without waiting for his father to answer. "Dad had nothing to do with it. To put it simply in terms you can relate to, his former mate is hell-bent on bringing about your demise in the most torturous manner possible. Once he opened the door to these dimensions, it also allowed her access. Because they built this world together, she has every right to manipulate your reality as he.

"The yin and yang of it is where the road ahead leads. Tony, Renée, Mom, Daniel, and most importantly you two, needed to experience more than your home three-dimensional reality you spent your lives in before you could deal with what comes next. You could look at all of what you have dealt with in the 1492 and 1942 realities as training to be able to move up to the next evolution of your consciousness."

Carl smiled with approval at how simple it seemed for his son to bridge the gap between him and the others. "There is a reason it took you and Alicia so many years to reach your obvious conclusion. Do either of you believe you would have ever consummated your love if it wasn't for the extraordinary circumstances you went through? Tony and Renée? The four of you have each spent centuries missing out on what was preordained from the beginning."

The second Carl finished, Sean and Alicia shared their minds again. This time they witnessed hundreds of lives over thousands of years, crossing every ethnic group imaginable. They realized that every time they found each other, the world always conspired to deny their love.

Every device in the history of unrequited love passed, each a dagger to their hearts as they re-experienced their former lives. One was either too poor, had too much color, had the wrong job in the wrong town, and most common thread of all, a fanatical drive to realize their individual potential. This repetitious point became all-encompassing where neither personality would submit to the other without the threat of losing that precious commodity.

When the journey reached their current lives, their consciousness separated. Both of them took time to digest the intensity of the experience.

Sean reached for Alicia and hugged her as if to let her go would mean to lose her all over again. When he finally did release her, he tenderly wiped away the tears streaming down her face with the back of his hand.

Carl continued. "Anthony and Renée have gone through exactly the same pain through their shared lives. One of the more positive aspects of what you all have endured is the opportunity to achieve the shared love denied to you. This is one of the reasons why I am risking all to end your suffering and allow your love to experience all that you are capable of sharing."

As another wave of emotions washed over her, Alicia needed to pause before she could respond. "Thank you for opening our minds to this. For years I could not understand what it was that held us back, and now it is so obvious."

This time when Sean went to comfort her, she waved him off. "I'm all right. Though it is an incredible experience to share our minds in all of those lifetimes, it now makes one-on-one conversation extremely awkward."

Alicia then remembered something. "Earlier you mentioned Daniel, as in Daniel Osaka? Why him?"

Carl smiled at Alicia's ability to not miss a thing. "If you look back, while you were on those emotional roller coaster rides, there was always someone around to steady you, give you comfort, keep you grounded, and sometimes bail you out of difficult situations."

Carl then addressed Sean. "You even referred to him as Father Osaka when you were about take the Decatur into Nipe Bay, Cuba."

Alicia chimed in. "I remember that."

She then directed her a question at both Carl and Sean Anthony. "Do you carry all of those voices in your heads all of the time?"

Sean wasn't ready to move on. "Excuse me, I may buy the part about our relationship to Tony, Renée, Rebecca, and Daniel, but somehow there is something much bigger involved. You could have dumped the six of us in different places and achieved the same results. So once again, why my ships?"

Alicia had figured out the answer. "Sometimes you can be so dense."

As the others shook their heads knowingly, Sean felt like the only one not in on the joke. "What?"

Carl reluctantly pointed to Sean Anthony. "For the most simplest of reasons. I needed a safe haven to have a family with Rebecca, which is something I never dared before. Unfortunately, the idea of a human half-brother did not appeal to Aaron, and that is when I lost him to his mother's manipulations."

Alicia laughed at her cleverness. "Seriously, do you carry all of the life you create around in your mind?"

Carl chuckled as he imagined ten thousand years of individual consciousness battling it out for the approval of the creator. "Not quite. Your collective memories are of a different nature than how I perceive things. Though it is true that I carry the memories of thousands of the life forms I have inhabited, they never encroach on my awareness. I along with others like me intervened to create all of life on planet Earth, so they are literally all mine to begin with, or ours. To top it off I can operate across a multiple of dimensions. To explain further would give everyone a headache. Unfortunately, because my former mate is every bit of this part as I am, she always had the ability to manipulate your gene sequencing to, shall we say, unhinge the lot of you."

"Because of the current lack of white hats in the world, she seems to be much better at it than you." Everyone froze at Alicia's frank assessment. "I'm just saying."

Carl nodded in agreement. "When you put it that way, I suppose you are right. Though in my defense, I did little to interfere because I always believed humanity's built in compassion would win in the long run."

"Please excuse my ignorance, but if there is an entire race of others like you that can create and destroy life across multiple dimensions, then how can a planet the size of a grain of sand in comparison hold so much interest to you?" Sean stopped as the situation reminded him of the one time he and his friends solved all of the mysteries of the universe while blazing on LSD.

"You see, and yet you are blind. Both you and Alicia spent your whole life fighting to maintain your optimism against a tidal wave of cynicism, yet you have lived merely a blink of my eye in time. Live long enough and everything becomes stale and corrupted. Evolution advances more from sheer boredom than a biological imperative, and perversely for one to risk all for something, anything new. I, my kind, and every other life form in this or any other dimension experiences exactly the same conundrum as they achieve different levels of awareness. Push forward or shrivel up and die. Shared love is the only exception to this. This is why I found it so fascinating how Rebecca and those she surrounded herself with fought so hard for all of these years."

Sean didn't wish to continue down this existential path. He needed to know what came next, so he asked Carl, "So where does that leave us?"

"Bottom line thinker to the end, eh? Okay, so here it is. You are going to represent all of humanity in order to help me recreate your world. In effect, you will serve as a template for the next evolution, and thereby save all life on this planet across every dimension under my authority. Can I get you anything to drink?"

Alicia noticed something that didn't sit well with her. "When you say you, do you mean that in the singular or the understood us?"

"Though everyone has a role to continue to play, the fate of this grand experiment will fall more squarely on one set of shoulders."

Before Alicia could confirm whom Carl had in mind, Sean wanted to establish a simple reality. "Why don't we start with where we are right now, and where Tony, Renée, and the rest of my command are?"

Carl spoke with his back to them as he poured from a bottle of wine. "I thought it was obvious. You are in the same world you appeared in at the end of 1941, however, it is now 2018, seventy-seven years later. This is the home Rebecca and I raised Sean Anthony in, and the reality closest in its societal makeup to the one you were born in. Though courtesy of Aaron, your home reality is in flux because a massive planetary disruption dissolved the molecular structure that bound everything together. As I said earlier, you are going to help recreate that reality's ecosystems."

Carl passed out the glasses. "First, let me reassure you again that both your ships and all of those who serve on them, including Tony and Renée, are safe for now. When all is done, either you will live a long and fruitful life, or all life in all realities on this planet will fade out like an old light bulb taking every moment of humanity into eternal darkness. So with all of that in mind, it is time to see exactly what you are made of."

Before either Alicia or Sean could question what Carl meant, the vacuum of space replaced the room they sat in. However, this was unlike any vision of space experienced previously in either book or film. Though still seated on the same couch, with Carl and Sean Anthony sitting in easy chairs across from them, surrounding them for as far as their eyes could travel were vignettes of events from their entire lives, real or imagined.

Before Sean could comprehend the meaning of any of it, he had his arms wrapped around a little girl who in her terror tried to climb out of the seat on a corkscrew roller coaster.

Alone in his quarters on the aircraft carrier USS Enterprise, Captain Anthony Knox discovered the communication system no longer functioned. He stormed out of the cabin into the corridor crammed with sailors rushing about as if they were under attack. Hoping what he had witnessed moments earlier on the flight deck had not actually happened, he grabbed the nearest sailor by the collar and demanded, "What the hell is going on?"

"No one knows, Sir, except everything is gone."

Tony grabbed him with both hands. "What do you mean gone?"

"Go see for yourself, Sir. It's all simply colors, with us sitting right smack in the middle, pretty as you please. Like stuck in the middle of some animated Disney movie."

Tony released his grip on the sailor and stood there for a moment confused. "Why would they move me from one part of the ship to another?"

"Sir?"

Without replying, Tony headed for the Admirals Quarters, reasoning that if he was still here, Sean and Alicia should be as well. His discomfort intensified when he found their cabin empty. Tony's normal reaction would be to rage his way to a solution; however, for the first time since Renée had died in 1942 this was all too much.

Thoroughly defeated, he slowly made his way down to the flight deck, shaking off the throng of sailors looking for someone of authority to make sense of the alien world around them. The crowd of sailors silently parted before him as he walked across the deck toward the same spot where he stood with Alicia and Sean moments earlier. By the time he reached the edge of the flight deck, hundreds of the crew crowded around him anxiously awaiting direction.

Emotionally numb, Tony stared at the colorful, swirling currents where the water should have been. Slowly he began to regain his equilibrium, and in doing so realized the USS Enterprise and the rest of the Task Force ships were literally sitting in the middle of a bubble roughly a mile in diameter. "Did someone drop us on some strange alien planet where the laws of physics don't apply?"

Tony looked up to the bridge to see it appeared empty. Scanning the ship's crew, his personal turmoil began to take a back seat to their needs. With Admiral Sean Phillips and his Chief of Staff, Admiral Alicia Calhoun missing, Captain Anthony Knox straightened up and addressed his crew. "It should be apparent to all of us that we are being tested. Tested to the limits of not only our perceptions of time and space, but tested as well in our bonds of loyalty to each other.

"Over the course of the last one hundred years, and across different realities the majority of you have performed well beyond the limits of normal human endurance, and for that you have my undying gratitude."

Tony then waved his arms around in a circle to emphasize the strange surroundings. "I am as much in the dark as the rest of you regarding all of this. However, we must not give in to despair and instead continue to stand in united defiance to the forces manipulating the very fabric of our reality."

As he sensed his words were having a positive effect on the assembled crew, Tony began to renew his sense of self. "Though most of you have not stepped back aboard the Enterprise in years, all of you need to return to your previous duty stations and await further orders."

At first no one moved, still unsure what to do. That is until a booming bass voice erupted near the bridge made it clear. "You heard the Captain. Get your asses back to your duty stations, *now!*"

The crowd of sailors rushed to obey the threatening command. As the deck cleared, Tony smiled when the tree of a man who backed up his order became visible. "Good to see you're still here, Thorny."

Commander *Thorny* Thornton, Commander of the elite SEALs deployed as a part of the Enterprise Task Force stridently walked over and stood next to him. He picked a cigar out of his pocket, lit it, and blew a smoke ring in Tony's direction. "Quite the cluster fuck, wouldn't you agree?"

"Situation normal. Is the rest of your team still onboard?"

"I haven't had time to find all of them, but I stationed those who I could throughout the crew on deck while you bullshitted them. Admirals Phillips and Calhoun?"

"Not here. Neither is Captain Aslan."

The nonchalant conversation belayed what both men were feeling, but years of history dictated their dance. "I'll head to the bridge; we need to get moving. At the least, it might create enough work to keep the crew focused. If you don't mind Thorny, see if you can round up enough of your SEALs and Marines to make sure no one tries to stir up trouble."

Unfortunately, as Tony delivered his orders to him, the man began to fade before his eyes. "What the hell Franklin? At least there was a semblance of sanity to your previous BS. So now you've reduced me down to two minute clips of useless nonsense?"

To his further frustration, everyone on the flight deck had also vanished. In disbelief, he spun around three times, each time expecting to find a different result, which considering the circumstances did not seem like such a crazy idea.

At the end of the third spin, Tony wound up back in the Admirals Quarters, but this time, he wasn't alone. On the couch sat the lover he thought he had lost, Captain Renée Aslan.

In his excitement at seeing her, Tony forgot all of the crazy as he rushed over to throw his arms around her. However, Renée abruptly stood up and her icy glare stopped him short. When he locked eyes, he could feel her mind bore right through him with an intense rage. If this wasn't disconcerting enough, the harsh judgment that followed betrayed a coldness Renée had never shown toward Tony before.

Frightened at what could have happened to cause this sudden change, he demanded, "What happened? Where did you go?"

"I didn't go anywhere." Her voice was as hard as the expression on her face. "You and everyone else were the ones who left."

The accusatory manner in Renée's voice chilled Tony to the bone. With a head full of worst-case scenarios to explain what had happened, the most obvious was the worst assumption he could make. "So what? You were gone for thirty minutes!"

"Maybe for you it was thirty minutes, but for me it was four hundred *years*," Renée stated with so much bitterness that Tony sank back onto the couch in shock.

Unmoved by his distress, Renée remained defiant. "After the first ten years waiting for you to return, I spent the next 390 years trying to forget you and everybody else I knew who ever existed."

Up to this point, every word she spoke yielded a grenade exploding in Tony's heart; her last ones felt more like a five hundred pound bomb. "Four hundred years?"

Without a response, Renée got off the couch, walked over to where Sean kept the Scotch and poured a tumbler full. With her back to him, the assault continued. "Four hundred years. Four hundred *years*." This time stated with more emphasis. "Believe me when I tell you how difficult it is to keep a clear image of someone in your head after the first fifty." She downed the Scotch and poured another without a thought to offer Tony any. "Then out of nowhere here you are again." This time there wasn't any emotion in Renée's voice as she downed her second drink.

Too devastated to react to this incredible news, Tony remained mute.

"What no snappy answer? No stamping of feet?" Renée filled the tumbler again, and sat down on the couch next to Tony. "So all of a sudden I am back on the Enterprise, and surprise surprise, alone with you." She shot down the Scotch and finished with a punch to Tony's gut. "I suppose Franklin put me here to save your ass, otherwise being here seems like a waste of my time."

Renée's onslaught finally brought Tony to the breaking point, and without any thought to the consequences, he lashed out. "How the hell could I know? Obviously living alone for all of those years has turned you into a real ball-busting shrew." Tony jumped to his feet and started to remove his pants. "Just in case, I'll make it easier for you to cut off my balls off and save us both anymore of this bitch fest."

The sight of Tony with his pants down to his knees trying to walk over to the desk for a pair of scissors was more than Renée dreamed of when had spent time rehearsing all of the ways to humiliate him if they were ever together again. Unlike Franklin's promise that Tony would see her again if he saved the Taíno, this was not true in her case. Franklin had made no such promise to Renée that she would see Tony again.

The sound of her laughter stopped Tony short. He slowly pulled up his pants, finished tucking his shirt in, and buckling his belt before turning around. "Okay, so were you truly gone for four hundred years, or were you instead studying at Joan Rivers School of Male Castration?"

Renée's laughter abruptly ended, and the insults returned. "You still don't get it. That I think it's amusing to watch you lose it, doesn't nullify everything I just said."

"This is going nowhere fast," Tony thought. "Fine if that is the way you want to play it, then this is how we will play it. You are currently onboard a United States Navy ship and I still outrank you. Therefore, since we are both in the dark about where everybody else went, why don't you get off your ass and head aft, while I go to the bridge to see if anyone else is still onboard."

Tony stormed to the door, but stopped short of turning the handle. "Better yet, since you're the one that has been around for four hundred years, you should be able to figure this mess out all on your own."

Renée's response was more violent than Tony was ready for, as a flying tumbler shattered against the bulkhead behind him, barely missing his head. Renée pushed her way past him and stormed out of the cabin, shouting profanities all the way down the empty corridor as she went.

Emotionally spent, Tony slowly made his way over to the bar. "At least she wasn't holding the bottle," he thought. He poured himself a glass and dejectedly sat down on the couch and waited. After finishing his drink, he decided to go to the bridge to see if anyone was there. He no sooner stood up to leave when Renée burst through the door angrier than ever. "What in the world are we supposed to do with that?" She obviously had gone topside.

Looking intently at each other, they came to the same conclusion. "*Franklin.*"

Renée began to pace the room like a caged lioness. "I know you are involved. Show yourself!"

Tony stood by quietly while Renée stormed around the cabin, calling out the avatar in every vile manner she could dream up. After ten minutes of futility, her emotional turmoil had reached its limit and she collapsed on the couch in despair, her hardness crumbled away in tears.

When Tony approached to offer comfort, she pushed him away. Her hostility toward him had not diminished. "You don't have the right to help. You lost that right years ago."

Tony frantically searched for a way forward, and after running through a few horrible responses settled on a Hail Mary. "Because that has always worked out so well for me in the past," he thought sarcastically.

Tony picked up the bottle, poured himself a stiff shot. "Blame me all you want if it makes you feel better, but from where I stand bitching incestuously about everything isn't working for you." Before continuing, he slammed down the shot. "Obviously, Franklin brought us together for a reason. Considering how much effort went into creating this Stanley Kubrick environment, one would think it's meant to prepare us for something even crazier to come."

Renée was not having any of the *we* in it. "You do realize that over the four hundred years you were gone, I didn't spend all that time alone pining for you. As a matter of fact, I entertained enough men and enough women to blow your mind."

The images this brought to Tony's imagination made him hesitate for a moment. Four hundred years leaves plenty to imagine. "And your point is?"

"After all of this, what makes you think there could be a reason that I still have any interest in you?" Then, in a nod to having read the visuals that had played across his mind, Renée chided, "You have *no* idea."

As emotionally crushing as Renée's comments felt, Tony stiffened his resolve to break through. "Regardless of the insanity that keeps pulling us apart that Shakespeare's most tragic characters would have a tough time matching, you still always come back to me. Why don't we start over with what you spent four hundred years doing, leaving out your many sordid affairs of course? There must be a reason Franklin felt it necessary."

Though the look in her eyes continued to throw darts at him, Tony noticed her body language had noticeably calmed.

Renée lifted her empty glass and shook it. "Pour me another drink."

Tony snapped to attention and saluted. "Yes Sir, Captain, *Sir*."

"You call me Sir again and you will find yourself floating in that chaos outside without a boat." Then to poke Tony one more time, Renée added, "And by the way, you have no idea *how* sordid some of those affairs were."

For the first time, the both of them cracked a small smile.

Tony decided a break was in order. "Give me a few minutes and I'll head to the mess hall and bring us something to eat. Try not to finish the bottle while I'm gone."

Renée looked at the bottle in her hand. "Not promising anything."

While Sean went on his wild ride, Alicia was back in her childhood home unwrapping a box to reveal a porcelain tea set her grandmother sent her, one of which arrived on her birthday every year until she was fifteen.

She looked at the cup, trying to understand the significance to her life. "Curious," Alicia thought. "This is exactly how I looked at these damn things every time they showed up." She then tried to remember to no avail a single conversation between her and the grandmother Alicia saw only three times before old age took her. "I knew so little about the family I came from. How could so much of that history disappear without a fight?"

Without a second to reflect further, Alicia occupied the woman's mind as a young girl. As she stared out a large bay window at the sight of falling snow, her grandmother raised her hand to reveal exactly the same teacup. To Alicia's shock, grandma shared exactly the same thoughts about the gift.

"Damn, how old were those cups anyway?"

Meanwhile, the little girl had disappeared from the seat next to Sean on the accelerating roller coaster as it dropped straight down with the tracks set to run out fifty feet below the car. The end of the ride would result in his impalement on the wrought iron fence he had unsuccessfully spent two weeks trying to paint for a neighbor when he was 15 years old.

Before he could react to his imminent demise, the roller coaster disappeared and he now sat astride his old dirt bike racing to catch up with one of his childhood friends. "Shit, this doesn't end well."

Sure enough, as he followed his friend who had disappeared over a rise, Sean shot into the air to discover the trail had made a sharp right turn, which left him nothing but boulders and the native chaparral as his landing site. "Broken collarbone, separated shoulder, a broken wrist, and the humiliation of being airlifted by helicopter to the local hospital," flashed through his mind.

Before he could crash, thankfully the cold hard metal of the bike became the leather of a horse saddle. Any relief Sean felt became short lived when he not only recognized the horse, but also that the thoroughbred was galloping out of control through the middle of a horse ring full of other riders. "Onondaga horse stables, really?" This memory also ended badly. After clearing the ring and two miles of crazy later, the horse abruptly came up short and simultaneously bucked hard to throw Sean high into the air. "Shattered tailbone, broken ankle, and a concussion."

Now half way up a sheer rock face without harness or rope, stuck in a crevice looking up at an impossible overhang, and shaking so hard from fear, he had difficulty maintaining his precarious hold. Through his much younger fear, Sean wryly thought to himself, "This is going to be a long day, if that is what you call this."

It took forever to revisit every one of his younger attempts to defy common sense. Though many ended in trips to the nearest hospital, there still were many others where the laws of gravity failed and the impossible achieved, though to his everlasting chagrin, none where others shared in viewing this success. "Thank god YouTube wasn't around back then. I would have never made it to fourteen."

Then the thrill ride abruptly ended with him on the bridge of his third command, the Ticonderoga class cruiser Port Royal deployed in the Arabian Sea. Sean remembered the day as though it was yesterday, while reading the decrypted message that informed him of the Twin Towers destruction of 9/11. "Go to General Quarters."

In a scene that felt as real as any others from their collected memories, Alicia sat on the Supreme Court bench as she cast her vote for the majority ruling in another of the landmark court's radical decisions that re-established the citizen's right to privacy. The secret courts, warrantless wiretaps, surveillance drones, police CCTVs, and all other forms of invasions would have to close their doors. Directly and indirectly, it would cost the nation over half a million jobs where the government paid Americans to spy on other Americans.

"What's next," Alicia thought. "Dragons are real, the Military Industrial Complex killed Kennedy, and Gracie and George Burns get to live forever?"

Not quite. Now in her early twenties, dressed in a gorgeous wedding gown, and with a much younger nervous Sean by her side, she thought, "This can't turn out well; no, not well at all."

"I couldn't agree more."

"Is that really you, Sean?"

"Apparently, you are on the same magical mystery tour as me," Sean replied.

Alicia threw the bouquet of flowers down and removed the veil from her face. "If you mean the type of magical mystery tour where nothing makes any sense at all, I guess so. What the hell do tea cups have to do with anything?"

"Tea cups?"

"Don't ask."

Before they could share any further thoughts, their minds once again became one, and their mutual visions returned to the thousands of memories of every star-crossed lover they had inhabited. This time the one common thread throughout the journey was each moment they managed to consummate their love for each other. They lost all meaning of time as thousands of memories came roaring in and out of their lives like a runaway passion train.

Then it was over as fast as it began. Sean opened his eyes to see Alicia next to him in their honeymoon suite bed in the Cambria, CA B&B. As he scanned the room, he noticed their strewn clothes were in the same place as before the green mist had transported them to the Enterprise Bridge in 2018.

Before Sean could react, Alicia threw her arms around him and passionately kissed him.

When Sean could finally come up for air, he asked, "What was that for?"

"You fought wars over me. My god, we are responsible for most of literature's tragedies."

"Yeah, and how about the time you sold me into slavery."

Alicia took a moment to recall the incident. "Yes, to save your life. As I recall, my dad wanted to hack you into little pieces when he found out the stable hand had taken my innocence. Errol Flynn had nothing on you. You were awfully reckless back then.

"Wait—, oh my god, selling you into slavery was Daniel's idea. Carl was right, he has been there all along."

With a start, Alicia realized their naked state and jumped out of bed to rapidly dress. "You do realize if they can pop in whenever they please, it stands to reason our private moments are not our own."

"Well, that sure puts a damper on any future intimacy."

The disappointed little-boy look on Sean's face at the thought of a life without sex amused Alicia. "Reality is a joke. Tony and Renée are god knows where, over ten thousand members of your command unaccounted for, and you have the time to worry about sex?"

She then remembered some of the deeper corners of his mind from when they had shared minds earlier, and the lightbulb switched on. "It's a miracle men get anything done."

Sean threw one of the pillows at her, but before it landed, they wound up dressed and back on the living room couch, but this time they floated in empty space with Carl and Rebecca seated across from them.

Too stunned to speak, and too mentally exhausted to care, Sean and Alicia didn't bother to question their current position.

Finally Alicia spoke, though not in her usual friendly tone. "Nice to see you again, *Rebecca*. So have you been complicit to Carl jumping us around like puppets on a string?"

Rebecca wasn't ready for the rebuke from her friend. "Honestly Alicia, and of course you Sean, I only recently found out about my past with Carl. Before then, I never knew him as anything other than the love of my current life."

Carl shrugged. "It was my pleasure to reveal to Rebecca the many lives we have shared together."

"Seriously, I hadn't a clue. I thought I married a career naval officer, not one of the progenitors of life on our planet. Believe me, it was quite the shock when he did his Mr. Spock mind meld for the first time. Remember, it was right before I tried to tell you he was in Specter's operating systems?" Rebecca wagged her finger at Sean and Alicia. "That'll teach you to doubt your resident mad scientist."

"None of this explains all of the craziness, and more importantly, why us, and why are you sharing all of this now?" No one could say that Sean lacked determination.

Rebecca jumped in before Carl could answer. "Because Carl figured out long ago that the only way to save humanity was to force us to evolve, which hasn't happened since he created us."

"Nothing new there," thought Sean. "By the way where did your son disappear to? At least he gave answers that didn't need an interpreter to understand."

"You met Sean Anthony?" Then turning to Carl, she demanded, "Yes *dear*, where is our son?"

Carl laughed at the sheer insanity that these people totally ignored that they were floating in space, and that they wanted to know about everything except that. "How fast they adapt," he thought before he answered. "Sean Anthony is busy elsewhere; however, since I will not get the most out of you until your curiosity is assuaged, here it is. I sent you into the 1492 reality as insurance against what could go wrong in the reality you were born in. I put Sean Anthony in your 2018 home reality to try to keep Aaron from using the President of the United States to destroy the world. With the help from, shall we say some unorthodox individuals, they managed to thwart Aaron's ultimate goal. However, he then sent the Greys, who consider humans an unwelcome virus, to deconstruct the 2018 reality into what you see below us."

Alicia wasn't happy to find out they were in the middle of what could only be described as a spitting war between superior entities. "This is right out of the Greek and Roman mythologies, down to the smallest details. Isn't this the part where you pull the curtain back and introduce us to Odin?" Alicia was plenty pissed off. "So with all life on Earth ended, will you send us to some other made up world, or will we wind up as specimens in some intergalactic museum?"

As Alicia finished her sarcastic retort, she finally noticed her new surroundings. The four of them floated a thousand feet over the alien world whose swirling mass of colors they had witnessed earlier with Tony on the Enterprise flight deck. Sean and Alicia floated in midair facing Carl and Rebecca.

Sean added a taste of Boris Karloff to his dialect. "Your laboratory?"

"Not funny Sean." Nevertheless, Alicia had to stifle a laugh.

"No, it is not." Carl needed to move things along. "We are above where the White House used to be."

With a wave of his hand Sean's chair disappeared, which sent him plummeting down to disappear into the swirling colors.

"What have you done?" In shock, Alicia struggled in vain to jump out of her chair to save him.

Carl eased Alicia's distress with a quick glimpse into Sean's current emotions. Instead of abject terror at the thought of his imminent demise, there was the excitement of a young boy seeing something wondrous for the first time.

❖

Fifteen minutes later, Tony returned with three bags full of food. "Not sure what you fancied, but since there isn't another living being on the ship, I figured what the hell."

Renée watched as he dumped the bags to reveal cooked chicken, beef, a variety of fresh fruits, and a selection from every dessert the ship's pantry carried. Over the next twenty minutes, they said little as they ate and drank their fill. An uncomfortable silence ensued between them after they finished the last of the meal.

More importantly to Tony, he noticed most of Renée's outward hostility had abated, so from a purely compassionate place, he reached out to offer comfort. Initially Renée pulled back, but recognizing her need, she gave in and embraced him. The second they came into contact, an even greater shock awaited them.

All at once, Renée's thoughts crashed like a wave into Tony's consciousness with everything she had experienced flooding into his mind, as his memories crossed over into hers. Along with this flood of information came the anguish she experienced repeatedly at being the only one left behind to shepherd an entire world toward the paradise it would become before her abrupt departure. The two years Tony spent alone in the Caribbean helping the Taíno paled by comparison.

Throughout the four hundred years of Renée's memories that scrolled across Tony's consciousness, he empathized with her rage toward not only him, but also Sean and Alicia. Franklin's warning that Renée could not survive outside of the 1492 reality that she had returned to from the dead only hardened her anger.

The worst of it played out in the first fifty years when she still held out hope they would return. He saw how at fifty years into her solitude, Renée decided enough was enough and began the arduous process of closing the door to her past life and everybody associated with it. Unfortunately, this approach left her unable to build anything permanent with those she spent the next 350 years dealing with.

As the memories caught up to their current predicament, Tony recognized why Renée chose to rage against him. Regardless of her wish to forget those she felt had abandoned her, Tony always remained in the back of her mind like a low-grade headache, which fed Renée's rage toward him.

Fortunately, for the both of them, when the last of the years finished playing out, their telepathic connection abruptly ended, and they both dropped unconscious to the floor.

As he slowly regained his senses, he noticed he was once again alone in his head. Through his blurred vision, the shape of Renée's face peered down at him. "So where are we now?"

She offered her hand to help him up, which he gladly accepted. When Tony once again tried to give her a hug, this time she rejected his advance by backing off. Unlike most instances where there would be confusion at this rejection, with Renée's memories still raw in his head he understood perfectly.

"So what now?"

Renée rolled her eyes. "You're asking me?"

"As I noted earlier, I figured after four hundred years you might have learned a few things. What does that ancient brain of yours think our options are?"

Renée picked up the nearest object she could find, one of Sean's books, and threw it at Tony. Before he could react, the book hit him squarely in the chest with enough force to knock him backward.

"Why did you do that?"

"The next time you use the word ancient and me in the same

sentence, it will be something else on your body that I aim for."

"*Obviously* that wasn't what I meant." Tony knew firing back at Renée was not going to help, so he tried a different tack. "Let's take a minute to try to understand what is going on. We are alone and back aboard the Enterprise. My question is, are we still in the 1492 Caribbean reality?"

Renée picked up the phone and offered it to Tony. "Why don't we ring the bridge and find out," she replied sarcastically.

Tony hit the bridge button and put the phone to his ear. "It's still dead." It was then Tony realized there were voices coming from the corridor. "We're not alone anymore."

Tony grabbed a reluctant Renée's hand and rushed her out the door.

The activity in the corridor mirrored the first time Tony entered it hours ago. He was about to grab the same sailor again, when a look and shift in mannerisms that reminded Tony of someone he should know replaced the panicked look on the young man's face.

"Nice to see you are looking much better than the last time we were together, Renée."

It dawned on Tony who was behind the young sailor's face. "Dr. Rebecca Cutler? How can you…?"

"In the flesh, thanks to a little help from Carl. Ensign Purser has been kind enough to take a back seat so I could give both you and Tony a little heads up."

Renée put up her hands in surrender. "And your inhabiting the body of someone else is supposed help us make sense out of any of this?"

"True enough, though unfortunately I would be a liar if I were to tell you the reason I'm here is to put either of your minds at ease."

"I preferred you with longer hair and minus the mustache." All Tony got for his attempt to lighten the moment was an awkward silence.

Rebecca gave him a sympathetic shake of her head before she

got to the point of her visit. "*Anyway*, as I have only a few moments, I need for both of you to listen up. You are back in the 2018 home reality, though home has gone through a bit of remodeling since you were last here."

Rebecca then abruptly threw her arms around Renée before she could object. Fortunately for her, Rebecca released her hold and took a step back to look her over. "Not looking too bad for a 500-year-old. How *do* you do it?"

This broke the ice, as Renée couldn't hold back her laughter at the absurdity. "After the first one hundred years you learn to roll with it. How long have you been gone, or am I the only one who was stuck playing God?"

Rebecca felt the anger seething beneath the surface in her friend. "You are one of a kind sweetie. Like your boy toy here, I only had a moment to catch my breath before coming here. We wanted to let you know that without your sacrifice there wouldn't be a world to come back to. We know it's a great deal to take in and we wish we could give you some time to come to grips with getting ripped out of your world, but unfortunately everything is coming to a head."

Then with a stern look toward Tony, she added, "So cut her some slack and don't be your usual insensitive reactive jerk."

Before he could utter a word to object, Rebecca turned her attention back to Renée. "Carl says to tell you that not only did you accomplish a miracle, but it was also the only way to keep you alive. You did an incredible job for such a freshly minted goddess."

Renée ignored the compliment. "You want to know the one thing above all others I learned over the four hundred years spent being all things to all people?"

The laconic manner in which Renée stated the question made Tony uneasy. "Maybe we should give her some time to adjust to coming back. Like for the rest of our lives?"

Renée ignored Tony's concern. "I learned that there are no gods, only those who derive a twisted sense of humor out of the suffering of those with more limited life cycles than themselves."

Renée then forced a smile for Rebecca. "What I want to do now is go back to my home."

The look on the sailor's face said it all. "I am afraid for the moment that will be impossible. Both of you need to see what is going on outside." Rebecca turned to head down the corridor.

Tony was about to argue they had already made the trip, but Renée began to follow, so he swallowed his frustration and joined them. When they reached the flight deck, Tony wanted Rebecca to explain why this latest insanity involved them. "You said we are back in our home reality, and if that is the case, what do all of those colors represent?"

She didn't disappoint. "I already told you. You are back home in the middle of the Chesapeake Bay, and those colors are a mixing bowl of every form of life and human construct on the planet at the molecular level. A demigod by the name of Aaron Fletcher, whose part in all of this I won't go into at this time, made a deal with aliens who then unleashed advanced disruptors that deconstructed everything into those beautiful colors all around the task force. It was only by Renée's efforts that the same did not occur in the 1492 reality. Though you couldn't possibly know it at the time, in doing so you also made it possible to save both the 1492 and 1942 realities in the process."

Renée backed off as it looked as if Rebecca was about to grab her again, but instead she placed one finger on Tony's forehead and one on Renée's. The flight deck disappeared, replaced by something right out of a Star Trek reboot. Their minds filled with a replay of the Grey's ships exploding in the upper atmosphere of Renée's 1492 reality world.

Rebecca withdrew her hands and the vision faded. "Unfortunately, there wasn't anything we could do to save this world, though as it turns out this might not be entirely the disaster it looks like. Actually…"

Rebecca stopped short, and turned her eyes upward as if listening intently to something, or somebody.

Tony waved his hands in a motion for her to finish the thought. "Actually what?"

Rebecca shrugged her shoulders in apology. "I'm sorry; I can't talk about that yet, too much information."

Tony returned his attention on the maelstrom that surrounded the ships and asked the obvious question. "Can you at least tell us what is keeping us from getting swept up into this mess?"

"No problem. That's why I'm here. When Renée returned, she came in with a portion of her 1492 reality around her. One of the perks of her becoming a goddess. As long as she is here, you and your ships stay protected in this bubble, at least for the moment. That is why we need to begin."

"Great! And I suppose next you are going to tell us where Sean and Alicia are."

"How astute of you Dr. Watson. They are in good hands and have received much the same information as I am giving you." Rebecca noticed the Enterprise Commanding Officer Captain Daniel Osaka approaching. "Explain everything I told you to Osaka to bring him up to speed. He is essential to all of this as well.

"For now Tony, rank makes you in overall command until Sean and Alicia return. However Renée, I cannot stress to you enough that you must remain aboard until further notice. If you leave, everyone and everything will deconstruct the second you do."

Confused, Tony asked Rebecca, "What crew?"

"Oh, sorry." She smiled, as the familiar shape of Commander Thornton and those who were working on the flight deck reappeared.

At that moment, Captain Osaka arrived. "Do either of you have an explanation for all of this?" Osaka's tone displayed a calm that was missing earlier.

Tony turned to Rebecca. "Ask her."

"Ask me what, Sir?"

"What you just told us, Rebecca." Tony didn't enjoy this game.

"Sir, my name is Ensign Ashton Purser."

Tony shook his head in frustration. "Would it be too much to ask for a conversation that covers all of the bases just once?"

"Imagine having to endure the same frustration with Franklin and Bowie for four hundred years." Renée had lost count how many times that her demands for information had gone unfulfilled.

Tony switched gears and addressed Osaka. "Captain, until we can figure out our options, we need to hold the crews together. You know the drill. We need to inventory our supplies to determine how long we can hold out. Hopefully, the idiots pulling our strings won't leave us hanging for too long."

"What about Admirals Phillips and Calhoun. They have always shown up at the right time." Osaka obviously would have felt better if they were the ones giving the orders as he recalled the event. "The last time they appeared on the bridge dressed in bathrobes holding glasses of champagne right before we joined up with the Missouri Task Force back from the 1942 reality, and then we all jumped into the 1492 reality."

"Understood Captain. However, Renée and I are all you have, so let's get our ships squared away."

Renée gave a heavy sigh, closed her eyes, and tried to will herself back to the home she had spent the last 120 years living in. When that didn't work, she mumbled, "Haven't I done enough already?"

Though he was worried about the effect Rebecca's news had on Renée, for the sake of everyone involved, Tony needed to find ways to minimize the impact of this hallucinogenic journey. "Captain Osaka, are we able to communicate ship to ship?"

"That's an affirmative, Sir. But may I ask where we are, and why does it look as if we are in the middle of a Claude Monet painting?"

The last thing Tony wanted to discuss with Osaka was another situation he didn't know enough about. "First, let's get control of the task force, and then we'll talk."

⎯◈⎯

Though Aaron carried the genes of both of his parents, Durius knew damn well he lacked the power to pull off the deconstructed mess by himself. "You do understand you have totally tied my hands by bringing the Greys in as you did. You have opened the door for both your brother and father to create whatever they want on this tiny piece of Hell. To the Continuum, deconstructed is 100 times worse than destroyed. What were you thinking?"

Durius had a personal score to settle. Her former partner Darius may adore the little simpletons, but Durius made it gruesomely clear that squashing them was her preferred interaction.

"It was either that or give up, and you know me well enough to know that giving up was never an option." Aaron's pathological hatred for all things human had always dominated his actions.

"Well, there is little left to accomplish here, so I am off to find out what your father is up to. Be a dear and don't do anything too stupid while I am gone."

Though he knew it would cost him, Aaron reacted as any other rejected son would. "What, like leaving the door wide open for him to recreate other dimensions that you can't affect?"

Surprisingly, the burst of rage he expected did not arrive; his mother's attention had shifted elsewhere.

"Or maybe something has arrived that we can use."

Aaron noticed it as well. "How could Dad bring them back here with the planet in this state, and still hold their form?"

With a voice dripping with deviousness, Durius agreed. "Why don't we go find out?"

With that shared thought, they both appeared over the Enterprise Task Force.

"How clever of the bastard. I don't know how, but he managed to splice another reality into this one. Honey, do your mother a favor and go see what's going on."

Aaron did not care for the idea at all. "You know how much I hate occupying one of those apes. It's humiliating."

"I need to know. Besides, if it wasn't for your lack of control, we wouldn't need to."

With one final look of disgust, Aaron began to sift through the chaotic minds of the Enterprise crew until he installed himself in the consciousness of a young female ensign. She happened to be close enough to Captain Knox to catch the last of his conversation with Captain Osaka. "Interesting, they don't know any more than us," Aaron thought.

With his consciousness still connected to his mother, she saw an opportunity. "I want you to stick as close as possible to this Captain Knox. I think we can use his ignorance to our advantage."

"More like rip his heart out and shove it down your throat," Aaron thought, before he responded submissively. "Yes Mother."

"Oh my," was the utterance Sean's mind formed at what could be described as the truth of innocence that all humans lose with age. With the force of a thousand superheroes, Sean's mind exploded onto a latticework of hyper-highways that shot off in all directions of space, just as he had imagined as a young boy. Interconnected within this network lay grand constructs the size of Earth's solar system, each one with a unique voice that called out to him as branches of his consciousness.

Through the center of Sean's euphoria, a puzzling foreign consciousness began to take shape. "I know where I'm going, don't be deterred."

"Is that me, or…" All of a sudden, he lay flat on his back in the middle of his childhood bed, sweating profusely from the one hundred degree, stifling summer heat and 90 percent relative humidity that filled the room. His feet ablaze without respite and his brain raging because his mother forced him into bed with the Sun still high in the sky.

The combination of the oppressive heat and years of neglected compassion drove Sean's mind back to the moment he realized how small his world had become. With this painful realization, panic arrived in the form of the claustrophobia one feels when trapped into a little box, a little box constricting at a rate where soon the last of his self-identity would be crushed.

Sean's rage intensified at this injustice, a rage that would have driven the vast majority of others into acts of brutality that lawyers would use in their closing arguments of their murder trial. Fortunately for Sean, he turned this negative energy into positive actions that repeatedly proved his self-worth, regardless of the cost.

This process continued in rapid succession as a series of other nightmarish vignettes of darkness and despair fought off each time with self-righteous determination. "Only one problem," Sean's memories vividly recalled. "I knew with each new attempt to strip me of my uniqueness that the cost would send me further away from remembering what my true place in existence was to begin with."

The alien voice in his head returned. "Rage replaces innocence and overwhelms curiosity, disrupting the ideas that made you different from all of the others. Where did you think all of your inner fortitude came from? Simply a fluke of nature? You might have given up altogether if left to your own devices, and I would have had to start all over again."

With an epiphany to end all epiphanies, the walls came tumbling on down. "Fifty years of questions trying to recapture something so extraordinarily simple and it was there all the time? How stupid can one person become?"

"Trust me, you were my only option. Your hybrid species doesn't churn out those with unlimited empathy by the bushel. Also, do you think it was merely your good fortune to be in Alicia's orbit?"

With a boatload of bitterness, Sean angrily answered, "It didn't help much that you hid away in the form of my younger brother to imprint me, and then stage your drowning when it came time to leave."

"I never left." The next images flooding his head were a succession of individuals who systematically altered Sean's road throughout his current life, always one at a time. One would take hold, explode old concepts, and then another replaced it when all insights were exhausted. Alicia and Tony were the only ones that stuck.

"Stuck," Sean winced. "That's right, I felt like I was running in place for so long. I knew my commission would be over as soon as the war game to test Specter concluded, and I didn't have a clue what would come next." This thought triggered the return of the little box, and the young boy in Sean felt the panic return.

However, with another mind-blowing explosion rending this reality asunder, the view returned to the grand construct with Carl by his side. "Through hundreds of lives with hundreds of Alicias, Anthonys, and Daniels to arrive at this place and time, I sincerely hope it doesn't take you as long to complete the next step. We don't have that much time for you to take."

⸻⬥⸻

After eating and drinking their way into oblivion, Tony and Renée fought off the urge to wait in the Admirals Quarters in the hope Sean and Alicia would soon return. Both realized after their many varied experiences dealing with the powers that controlled their movements that it would be a waste of time.

For once, Tony went for the lesser of spirits and grabbed a bottle of Chardonnay as well as a bottle of Scotch before they left to return to their old cabin aboard the Enterprise. When they arrived, Tony poured two glasses of wine and handed one to Renée. "You ready to talk about it?"

"Talk about what? Like how it felt to live while those I grew to love shriveled up and died until it got to the point it was either learn how not to care or put a bullet in my head? How every morning I would wake up and hope that today was the day you would come back and life would return to normal? And when it didn't, either spend the day curled in a ball helpless to perform the most rudimentary of tasks or go change the lives of those not responsible on a whim?" Renée's words laid bare the bitterness she carried.

Tony tried to sympathize. "I can't imagine…"

"No you can't, so it's pointless to try." Renée aggressively downed the wine and handed the empty glass back to Tony. "I know we have something stronger."

"Maybe we should wait until after we meet with the rest of the senior officers." It wasn't lost on Tony the irony of him trying to be the calming influence.

As if she had read his thoughts, Renée drove this point home. "I have a better idea. Why don't we make believe none of what we do matters anyway and blow the fleet to shit instead. Pour me a real drink and shut the hell up for a change."

Defeated, and without any other options, Tony picked up the phone to confirm with Osaka that the senior commanders were aboard, only he found the phone dead again. "Will you be all right alone? The phone is not working, so I need to go to the bridge."

Renée merely shook her head as she headed to the cabinet for the bottle of Scotch.

Tony hurried out of the cabin and headed for the bridge. "Odd," he thought. "Why haven't I run into anyone and where is the Marine who is supposed to be on duty?"

His answer came when he opened the door to find Benjamin Franklin alone on the bridge with his hands randomly pushing the buttons on the console. "Hello again, dear friend. Awfully sorry about Renée's state of mind, but couldn't be helped."

Tony ignored him and looked out the window. In horror, he watched as the rest of the ships of the Task Force sank into the mass of colors, the barrier that held back the chaos no longer in effect. "What is happening. Are you responsible?"

"Out with the old and in with the new."

The cavalier manner in which Franklin stated this ended whatever restraint Tony had left as he charged his tormentor with his fists ready. However, he passed through Franklin to crash awkwardly onto the deck.

"Now, now my dear fellow. I hoped by now you would have a little more faith in me. In this reality, all of these ships and people are a hindrance to what must come next. Only you, Renée, and Daniel matter." As Franklin finished, bottles of wine and Scotch appeared on the console along with three glasses.

Before Tony could respond, the door opened and Renée entered with her side arm, which she proceeded to empty in Franklin's direction. Unfortunately, the only items she managed to kill were the bottles, glasses, and one of the ship's control panels. Renée slowly sank to the deck, visibly spent. "Why can't you just die?"

Franklin calmly walked over to her and gently removed the weapon from her hand. "Though it is nigh impossible to end my existence with your silly little popgun, you can still end poor Tony over there."

When he saw the gun, Tony dove under the nearest cover and now tentatively peeked out to see if it was safe. "You could have killed me. What were you thinking?"

Looking first at Renée and then Tony's precarious state, Franklin slowly shook his head in disapproval. "It seems I must expedite matters." With these words, the Enterprise Bridge began to dissipate around them. As the carrier slowly disappeared, Renée grabbed the gun from Franklin, slammed in another clip, and emptied it in the direction of his head.

This time there were no walls to amplify the sound of the exploding gunpowder or the projectiles hitting steel bulkheads. Tony and Renée appeared in the middle of a pasture along with Franklin and a surprised Daniel Osaka.

However, the currents of rushing colors remained a mile away all around them.

"What the hell?" Osaka cried out.

"You my boy are about to have a come-to-Jesus moment – literally." As Franklin spoke Daniel disappeared in a puff of green mist.

Left without his cover, the silliness of his position crouched in the pasture made Tony laugh, until he saw the look on Renée's face while still holding the smoking gun.

Tony then turned to Franklin. "You do realize that you are going to get me killed, and if it happens at the hand of the woman I love..." Tony stopped and shook his head. "I guess there isn't a damn thing I can do about it."

Franklin smiled in response and pointed behind Tony.

Tony turned around to observe the colors rapidly overtaking the pasture.

"You better keep up with her, or you will find out what it will be like to be part of the chaos outside."

Tony whipped around to see Renée running in the opposite direction. "What the hell? Where is she going?"

With urgent prompting from Franklin, Tony took off after her. After a couple hundred yards, a beautiful modern ranch style home came into view.

Renée stopped short, and turned back to face him as he covered the distance. "This is my home in the Rockies, or at least an exact replica. Right Franklin?"

The front door opened with Franklin slowly peeking out. "Are you going to keep shooting at me?"

"That depends. Real or replica?"

This was not at the top of Tony's list of questions. "Wait a minute. None of this, the crazy colors or if this is your home, matters as far as I am concerned. What happened to my ships and crew?"

Franklin uncovered from the door and walked out onto the porch. "They are all fine. I returned them to their collective. Over a third of them are buried deep in both of your subconscious because they have the same imprint as you."

"That wasn't the answer I expected." Tony could see Renée was about to explode again, so he did what any sensible man would do when confronted with a raging mate armed with a gun, he got out of the line of fire. "Why don't you answer Renée's question."

"We are standing at an elevation of 6,200 feet above sea level in a valley you call Jackson Hole, Wyoming, which I must admit is rather striking in its beauty."

Renée reloaded the pistol. "I may not be able to put a dent in your sorry ass, but it sure feels good trying."

"I guess I can't blame you for lacking a sense of perspective about how things have turned out, but at this moment I can say unequivocally that you two have sacrificed more than anyone, including me, has a right to expect. Therefore, I have placed you in a shelter from the storms that rage around you from every corner of your reality." Franklin then bowed down gracefully, upturned eye and impish grin begging sincerity. "You are very welcome."

This only heightened Renée's anger to the point she once again emptied the clip in a tight pattern directed at his groin. "What have you done to my world you clownish oaf?"

Franklin didn't skip a beat at the ineffectual assault. "Because of your perseverance and fortitude, the world you ruled over is still the same as when you left."

Franklin then dropped his mask of joviality and became deadly serious. "This little patch of land, the world of the Taíno, and the world of 1942 that Rebecca inherited is still very much in perfect harmony, and that is why you both have earned a respite. A respite that only you can decide to end, or for as long as those who harness the power to command the nature of this realm."

"What if all I want to do is go back home to where the view from here stretched for miles?" In disgust, Renée holstered her gun and disappeared into the house.

Tony went to follow, but Franklin motioned for him to stop. "There is more."

"There always is with you." Tony walked past Franklin and continued to the door.

"The something more is that either you or Renée can with a mere thought summon any of those you wish into your presence, at least any of those who belong to your respective imprints."

Tony stopped short and turned around. When he did, next to Franklin stood SEAL Commander Thornton, who wasted no time getting to the point. "Where the hell are we, and where the hell is my command?"

Tony closed his eyes and cleared his mind of everything but Renée. When he opened his eyes, Thorny was gone. "Real? Or more ghosts like you?"

"Real enough to bleed if Renée shoots one of them." Franklin reached into his coat pocket, pulled out his pipe, and began to fill it from his tobacco pouch. After he lit it and took a puff, he pointed it at Tony. "She will forgive you in time."

Franklin's segue caught Tony off guard. "Not as long as she equates me with you and how she was abandoned. I don't see it. That's too many lifetimes to overcome."

He smiled at Tony's ignorance. "I would be more worried if she was indifferent. With a little time alone, I think you might have learned enough by now not to screw up an opportunity when you see it."

Tony took a minute to think about what Franklin said before he asked, "So you are doing us a favor? And of course you have a reason that I am sure involves Sean, Alicia, Rebecca, Carl, and apparently Daniel Osaka, all of whom are nowhere to be seen."

Franklin shook his head in agreement. "They don't share your imprint, therefore as explained earlier, no access. Sean is experiencing his particular brand of awakening at this very moment. The decisions he and Alicia make will dictate exactly what choices, if any, there will be for the future of your species and its place in this part of the galaxy."

"And I am not important enough to be a party to this, so stick me in an out of the way location like a love sick teenager?"

Tony's dive into self-pity angered Franklin. "Sometimes I want to smack you. Before I planted your ass in 1490 Cuba, you had already checked out, yet within a year with the Taíno, you regained all of your former piss and vinegar. That is how Renée came back to you, and that is why she had to be the one left behind. So here you are again with your manhood challenged, yet where are you both? Together again, only this time with no one around to screw it up, including me. So stop asking stupid questions and get your ass into the house." Franklin finished with a smack to the back of Tony's head.

"How long?"

"Do you believe Renée was gone for four hundred years?" Franklin wiggled his finger back and forth. "You might think it's a day or ten thousand years. It all depends on how you live from here on out. My advice to you would be to choose wisely."

Before Tony could object, a blanket of green mist enveloped Franklin and then exploded with a flash. After starring at the chaos surrounding him for a few minutes, he entered the house and shut the door behind him.

⌁

I especially relished the part where you made the impossible promise – classic misdirection." Bowie hit the rewind button and Franklin's speech to Tony replayed.

Franklin didn't share his friend's interpretation. "Personally speaking, I hope they make it."

"This coming from the one who predicted when they still lived in caves that they would kill themselves off fighting their conflicting nature thousands of years ago. Besides, there is not a single thing either you or I can add until called upon."

Bowie bent over the glass table and hoovered up three thick lines, then violently shook his head. "So, I've got some material I want to try out, so why don't we turn this freak show off and go have some real fun?"

"Whatever. Why don't you grab Iggy and drag him along. After all, he is better suited for that crowd." Franklin continued to view the ranch house, and with a click, zoomed inside to find Tony alone in the living room. Renée remained behind her closed bedroom door, an out of bounds location even for Franklin's prying eyes.

"If I didn't know you better, I would say you've acquired a soft spot for your pets." Bowie had the perfect present for Franklin as two German Shepherds appeared on both sides of him.

Most disconcerting to Franklin was that their faces shared similar traits to Tony and Renée. "Ha-ha." With a wave of his hand, they disappeared along with Bowie.

Franklin was surprised when he turned his attention back to the monitor and found Tony had a female guest he recognized. He unmuted the sound and the conversation filled the room. "Oh my, this *is* a problem."

Shortly before Franklin had appeared aboard the Enterprise, Aaron felt the rush of thousands of lives vacating the ship, including the body he inhabited. This left him no other choice but to rejoin his mother, where they watched the ships disappear.

Durius had sensed Franklin's arrival. "Why is he here, and what has he got to do with this?"

Aaron didn't understand. "If you know he's here, how come he didn't notice us?"

Before answering, Durius gave Aaron a look that said, *how is it possible you are my son?* "Your dear old daddy imported a bit of reality from another dimension with those ships in it. Therefore, we can see in, but he can't see out."

Durius felt the energy move off to another location, which they followed. "He took three of the humans with him. I have an idea, but it doesn't include you. You go ahead and play with the Erganats, and I will fill you in later when I need you."

This suited Aaron fine, because at this point he didn't care. "If Mother doesn't care for the way I handled events, then maybe it's time to find out if she can do better."

⸻◆⸻

While experiencing a myriad of sensory overloads, Sean continued his hypersonic journey. The voices along the way became more insistent for him to learn what they had to offer.

"You never did find out a single truism about the family that came before you. All of the answers are in here for the asking." This voice seemed vaguely familiar, yet irritatingly slightly beyond recognition similar to trying to hold onto those fantastic dreams when after you wake up.

"You never were able to get justice for the time your teacher Mr. Pruss laughed when Rudy sucker punched you. Do you want know what karmic justice finally caught up with him? Come on in and see."

It wasn't only the slights that Sean experienced. Next along his memory tour, came the jolly Mrs. Ringo, who settled Sean down enough to sit in kindergarten. Then the gentle soul of his second grade teacher Mrs. Heller, who read from Charlotte's Web that brought a wave of emotional beauty that Sean relived throughout his entire life. Finally, the voices of Mr. Massey, Mrs. Fletcher, and his advisor Mrs. Glass who moved mountains to ensure Sean's appointment to the Naval Academy; they all beckoned.

The pull of these memories began to act as an anchor to slow his forward progress, which stopped abruptly when the one sideshow he could not escape arrived as a bolt from the blue. "Hello lover; it's been a long time."

"So what are you going to tell your parents about us?" Sean repeated the words verbatim from 1974, as he lay in the same bed with Angela's soft body wrapped in his.

"What makes you think I would tell them anything? I'm off to Berkley in three weeks, and we will never see each other again."

The words that came from her lips devastated him for months. "After what we have shared over the last six months, you don't love me?"

"Love you? I'm on a full ride to Berkley, and you are a few dollars away from sleeping in your car. What kind of future is that? I needed someone to lose my virginity to before I left highschool, and you were the most experienced male who was available. You're cute and all, but really?"

Sean was incensed. "Well, I went to college and rose to the rank of Admiral. You call that no future?"

"And I was supposed to read that from the wreck of your highschool achievements, and that you had no home life? No thank you."

Angela stuck her hand under the sheets to reach between Sean's legs. "Forget about all of that." Angela climbed on top and placed her breasts inches from Sean's face as she slowly gyrated her hips. "How about something new," she purred in his ear.

Recoiling in horror, Sean pushed her off and jumped out of the bed. Before his feet could hit the ground, he found himself in another vaguely familiar bed. "Sally? You're the one who gave me mono."

Thus began a parade of women, each naked in another bed in another place, each one gave a Sean piece of their soul, only for him to manipulate them in return. Twenty years of a complete accounting of those women who paid the price for Angela's rejection of the love-starved Sean.

The voice railed sharply in Sean's head. "How can you hope to know the truth you seek if you keep reliving failed experiences, and using these memories as reminders of who you shouldn't be instead of who you have grown to become?"

Sean rose to his defense. "I used empathy to pray on their dreams. How else could I ensure I evened the scales for my actions, but by giving all I could for the rest of my life to those who needed it?"

"There is a fine line between empathy and self-immolation, or to call it as it truly is, hubris. In working so hard to shelter others, you act as a god, yet your actions stop you cold on the road to becoming one. Ironic wouldn't you say?"

All of the pent up frustration Sean had experienced throughout his life about never being good enough, never living up to his lofty self-expectations hit home with another flash of enlightenment.

The rooms faded, and Sean once again traveled through space, however, this time he flowed at an incredible speed with a natural easiness of manner. "How could I not have seen that sooner?"

The voice in his head laughed. "And we have only begun. Then Alicia."

"What about Alicia?"

"Not quite yet." Then the voice announced threateningly, "First, *The Night of the Living Dead.*"

"Shit."

Left alone with Rebecca after Carl disappeared when Sean sunk into the swirling mass, Alicia was at her wit's end. "How can this happen. What's next Rebecca, are you going to turn into a dragon and carry me back to your lair for lunch? Where did Sean and Carl go? And what are we supposed to do, float around until they return? That is if they do return. Someone better give me some sanity quick. I'm done with being led around like a drugged rat in a maze."

"I wish I could help you understand Alicia. All I can say is whatever Carl is showing Sean is bigger than either one of us can imagine. Honestly, Carl showed me only enough so I would trust what he was doing."

"How do you know? I mean, what do you actually know? Only after dragging all of our asses all over time and space did Carl come clean with you. Hell, he could be creating illusions for some other sick purpose." Alicia then realized she was back in the strange room from earlier, seated next to Rebecca on the couch.

"Thank goodness we are back home," Rebecca sighed with relief. "Oh hello Sean Anthony. I didn't know you would still be here."

Sean Anthony ignored his mother and addressed Alicia. "Dad is trying to give Sean a gift greater than any human has received, including the gifts he gave the likes of Copernicus and Einstein. Can I pour you two some wine?"

Though usually pragmatic, Alicia intentionally continued to argue aggressively. "Provided I still believed all of this is actually happening, I fail to see any grand plan in Carl's manipulations of time and space. The bit about shared consciousness could merely be drugs accompanied with a cheap parlor trick that is being recorded like some sick reality show."

Sean Anthony's first inclination was to allow Alicia a glimpse into his mind, but thought better of it. "If only life was that simple. In a reality where everything and anything that the human species is capable of imagining came directly from its biological connection to Carl and five others from the Continuum, the hope was humanity would evolve from this to greater ideals and deeds.

"Unfortunately, after ten thousand years of stagnation, at the rate humanity is currently plundering the planet, extinction within the next two hundred years became obviously apparent. I can show you a million logical scenarios for what is taking place, but you can as easily dismiss all of them if you are convinced of some sinister mind game. From that perspective, it would be useless to argue the point."

Sean Anthony paused to pour wine into three glasses. "Every action and counteraction taken by despots to control the planet's wealth has distracted your race from its true potential. Instead, humanity treated every technological advance we provided in an effort to force evolution, as yet another weapon to feed the greed. You can't establish a colony on the moon, but you sure can put tons of trash in orbit. You can smell the stink way out in space. Even without Durius' intervention, Dad would have eventually deconstructed the planet himself."

Alicia was puzzled. "Durius, I have heard that name before."

Sean Anthony handed his mother and Alicia each a glass. "Yes in the Spanish dungeon. Darius and Durius were mates."

Still puzzled Alicia asked, "And Darius?"

"Sorry, Darius is Carl." Sean Anthony then asked Alicia, "Aren't you every bit as disgusted with your brethren as Dad? If you were honest with me, you wouldn't care less if one monumental act cleaned up the whole mess. Let's face it, sitting back and enjoying the ride seems to be your best option."

Though Sean Anthony's words managed to clear up some of Alicia's confusion and smooth the rough edges of her emotions, she wasn't done yet. "I obviously can't argue with you about the mess we have made of the planet, but without understanding why we were the ones chosen, you all remain suspect. I won't stop questioning the motivations of others, even if they come from a superior alien race that helped create me."

Sean Anthony thought hard for a moment before changing tact. "What do your instincts tell you about Mom?"

"If I were to have a daughter, I imagine Rebecca as my ideal of perfection."

Rebecca interrupted. "That is so sweet of you to say." She then reached over to give her a hug, which this time Alicia gladly accepted.

After gently untangling herself from Rebecca's embrace, Alicia continued. "How is it that after a lifetime of colliding with thousands of individuals, and finding only one who shared enough of who I am to maintain a close relationship with, how is it possible that all of a sudden I find myself surrounded by kindred spirits? How can any of this be real?"

Rebecca gave her opinion. "Where I have never questioned my single-minded pursuit of scientific enlightenment, as I became close to both you and Sean, I discovered how multifaceted you both are. You crave the big picture, so of course no single idea or concept is going to fulfill your hunger. Carl sees this in you, along with your drive to evolve. That puts you in some extremely exclusive company. Sitting back on a porch and reliving past successes as a reward for a life well lived would be your vision of Dante's inferno."

Sean Anthony knew to continue along this thread would amplify Alicia's frustration. He stood up, walked over to the hall closet, and pulled out two jackets, one of which he handed to Rebecca.

Rebecca put the coat on and pointed back at the closet. "Grab one for Alicia. By the way, where are we going?"

"I think it's time to see what a world that expresses your most cherished dreams looks like. Let's take Alicia for a stroll through our world, the one she helped bring about in 1942?"

"That is a great idea, and can we stop by your house so I can see Lydia?"

"Of course," Sean Anthony answered, as he handed Alicia her coat.

Alicia remained seated, as she laid the coat by her side. "I'm not going anywhere until you tell me what happened to Sean."

Regardless of her obstinate stance, Alicia now stood in the front yard wearing a buttoned up coat. She could see, as well as smell and hear a distinct difference in the surrounding environment. "What a beautiful place you've chosen to live in."

Rebecca stifled a laugh. "No different than anywhere else on the planet. Massing people on top of others ended the minute the population declined to less than four billion worldwide. That, along with ending the need for protection and the corresponding massive military forces, people readily accepted the peace and tranquility living without borders brought to their lives."

It was Alicia's turn to stifle a laugh. "It sounds as though you drank the Kool-Aid. Where is everybody, and why not zap us there like every other time without asking *do you mind* first?"

As if on Sean Anthony's cue, a circular craft appeared in the sky directly overhead and silently settled on the street in front of them. "It's better to observe this world up close and personal."

"Where did that come from, and how is it so quiet?"

Rebecca grabbed Alicia's arm and walked over to the alien looking craft. "Normally we would call ahead, but apparently Sean Anthony wanted to show off. It's a different application of the same technology as Specter, environmentally clean electromagnetic pulses instead of combustion propulsion. Carl and I had a hand in developing it to replace automobiles."

As they approached, a door on the side swung open and music Alicia remembered sharing with Sean over thirty years earlier spilled out. "Are you shitting me? Television's Marquee Moon album? No one knows about Tom Verlaine. Sean spent hours trying to convince me of his musical genius."

Alicia turned to Sean Anthony, her hackles up. "Will you stop screwing with my mind?"

Sean Anthony smiled. "Sorry to disappoint you, but in this world he ranks up there with all of the musical greats. You'll hear several bands that made major contributions, yet remained obscure in your personal history." To punctuate this, *In for the Kill* by the 1970s power trio Budgie followed.

Rebecca moved to the chords as she entered, Alicia tentatively followed, and Sean Anthony brought up the rear as he continued. "Music rules this world, good teachers are the celebrities, and the only carbon footprints are those made when you step on a plant."

As Alicia settled into her seat, the craft silently rose vertically into the air. After it cleared the surrounding trees, the craft rapidly picked up speed as it transitioned to horizontal flight.

The interior maintained the circular shape as the outside, with the seating in a half circle hugging the wall. Alicia was about to ask what the monitors placed at eye level that ran all the way around the inside were for, when the outside world opened up in a breathtaking display.

The 360-degree view showed a rolling landscape, populated with Ash trees in all their fall majesty and stretching as far as Alicia could see. "Eastern United States?"

Taking on the tone of a tour guide, Sean Anthony began to narrate the scene below. "Correct, except the concept of the United States no longer exists, and the Washington D.C. area remains a swamp. In New York, the world's only form of central government exists solely to keep the never ending conflicts in the Middle East from affecting everyone else."

Rebecca jumped out of her seat to point excitedly to the east where the Atlantic Ocean came into view. "And that is New York."

Though the Statue of Liberty and general layout of the city remained familiar, Alicia noticed the scale had unmistakably shrunk in size. The Empire State Building dwarfed every other high-rise on the skyline, and they looked pre-WWII in age. "Did the world stop putting up buildings? How do the oligarchs measure their dick size?"

Sean Anthony laughed at the reference. "I guess in the bedroom where it belongs."

"Sean Anthony!" Rebecca smacked her son on the shoulder and apologized to Alicia. "I am sorry to admit he got his foul mouth from me. But seriously Alicia, when we ended WWII over seventy years ago, we instigated a worldwide contraception program."

"How did you convince religious institutions and big business to buy into neutering future consumers?" Alicia found it impossible to believe that any power could reign in centuries of bad behavior so fast.

"Funny you should ask. With the Vatican, all it took was to show a video of the atomic bomb we dropped on Russia along with the promise we wouldn't do the same to the Vatican in exchange for a vision from God to convene the second Council of Nicea. You might say we packed the council with reformists who not only preached the sanctity of Mother Nature, but also brought women into the clergy. Pope Alexandria is the second female pope since. It's amazing when women are given a real choice about their bodies, how fast they find having a gaggle of children for a living loses its charm."

As she finished, the vehicle stopped its forward flight and began to settle in the middle of Central Park. Only this version of the park was without the ring of tony apartments Alicia would have used to identify the place. Seconds after landing the door swung open to reveal a small group of people waiting outside.

One particularly beautiful woman stood out from the rest and was the one Rebecca rushed over to hug first. "I've missed you."

Rebecca looked around, and in disappointment asked the woman, "Where's Lydia?"

"Sorry Mom, school takes precedence, even over a visit from her grandmother." The woman untangled herself from Rebecca's grip, walked over to Sean Anthony and gave him a quick kiss, before turning to address Alicia. "You must be Alicia. Mom has told me all about you. I am Phoenix Eddington, Sean Anthony's wife, and currently President of the World Council. Welcome to New York."

Left with no one to talk to, and unsure about how much space to give Renée, Tony wandered around her home, and after checking it out thoroughly, concluded it best not to touch anything. "I suppose this is the kitchen because it has counters. But where's the refrigerator?"

"Right where it belongs stupid." To his amazement, a door to his right slid back where previously there was no door. To top it off, the voice was a replication of his.

This was too much for Tony, who turned to leave.

"If you are not going to get anything, close the door, you're wasting energy, fool."

Frustrated, Tony returned to the living room where he went straight for the Scotch, poured a stiff one, and plopped down on the couch. "I wonder if the TV works."

Before he could begin to figure it out, one of the most beautiful women he had ever seen appeared out of nowhere two feet away on the couch. Surprised, Tony launched the contents of his drink all over his shirt and pants.

If not for the severely open cleavage, Tony would have noticed that she was dressed in a white summer dress with lavender, red, and blue flowers scattered randomly, with shoes to match. Emerald green eyes, porcelain white skin, and a face framed with the darkest black hair finished off her striking appearance.

"Sucks being you right now, doesn't it?"

A thousand ideas rushed through Tony's mind as he tried to determine who and where this creature came from. "Who are you and what are you doing here?"

Durius slid closer and through pouting lips seductively whispered in his ear. "Whatever you want me to be tiger, not like that shriveled up old man that is leading you around by your dick."

Something in this woman began to trigger an uncontrollable feeling in Tony he hadn't felt since a teenager. He jumped to his feet before all rational thought escaped him. "Excuse me for a moment; I need to clean up this mess." Under his breath, he mumbled, "Forget the glass next time, and simply bring the bottle."

"You know you have only half of the story, the half that keeps putting you in situations contrary to your needs. Why do you tolerate it?"

After a healthy pull from the bottle and a moment to let the scorching pain in his throat subside, Tony regained some of his self-control. "To tell you the truth you remind me of Disney's portrayal of Wicked Queen Grimhilde. Honestly, do you have a spell you use, or do you come by this ultimate seductress routine naturally?"

"Not there yet," he thought, so another long pull from the bottle ensued.

A look of disgust crossed her fantastical visage. "Why is it that such a magnificent example of a human warrior is sitting on his ass while earth shaking events unfold without you? Have you lost yourself so completely to the whims of someone who can only think of herself that you would sacrifice all of who you truly are?"

"Who says I am doing anything of the kind. You don't know anything about…" Tony stopped short and gave her a hard look. "Whoever you are, what I see is you attempting to drive a wedge between me and Franklin, which can only mean you are one of those we are fighting against."

"Don't be such an idiot. Do you think this Franklin is looking after anyone's best interests but his own? Let me show you who he is and what he represents." Durius pointed to a spot on the wall and an alien landscape popped into view. Within the landscape, two reptilian creatures lounged on the shore of a beautiful lagoon. "You know these two as…"

Before she could continue, they both heard the doorknob to Renée's bedroom door turn. In a panic, Tony turned to Durius and discovered she was gone. When he turned back to the wall, the alien landscape too had disappeared.

Renée stood in the doorway with her arms crossed. "Who were you talking to?"

Rather than try to talk about the strange encounter, Tony decided it would definitely complicate an already sensitive situation. "Apparently just my imagination. Are you hungry? I am hungry, and I'll be damned if an automaton that sounds like me feeds me. What gives with that anyway?"

For the first time since she reunited with him, Renée smiled. "You might have noticed he sounds like a jackass."

"Hard to miss."

With the realization that this portal was wide open into another reality she had previously lacked access to, Durius jumped at the opportunity "Let's see how he likes it when I crash the party."

Franklin paced the floor in Tony's Cuba house while loudly gesticulating wildly over what had happened. "How could she show up there? It is not possible without them knowing about it." He paced some more and contemplated the possibilities. "Maybe it wasn't her. If it was her, everyone would have known. That woman can't make a move without everyone knowing."

A half an hour later he still paced, when clarity abruptly arrived. "She wasn't there, she was here, that's how."

"It took you long enough. I knew there was a reason it took your kind over 200 million years to evolve; though only the two of you managed it."

In fear of the woman, Franklin struck up a defensive pose. "You used their sanctuary as a portal. How could we have missed this possibility?"

"Because unlike my former husband, who has a weakness for using fools like you to further his agenda, I always preferred a more hands on approach." Durius glanced around the room unsatisfied with what she did not see. "Where is that twisted cousin of yours?"

Thinking frantically on his feet, Franklin threatened, "As soon as we realized you were with Tony, he went to warn Darius. They will be here any second with other members of the Continuum to penalize your rash action."

Without making a move toward Franklin, Durius simply smiled as a hundred knives in full flight appeared out of nowhere and slammed into Franklin's body. "You should know better than to lie to me lizard breath."

Though extremely painful, Durius made sure none of the blades were fatal, so when she walked over and used her hand to drive one of the knives deeper into one of his many wounds, Franklin writhed in agony.

"Seriously, where did he go?" Before he could answer, she chose another strategically placed knife and this time slowly twisted it back and forth. "Or is he still slumming around on this world?"

Through the excoriating pain, Franklin knew he could not continue to take the torture, so being the pragmatic 200-million-year-old survivalist he was, he abandoned his guardianship over this reality and by extension the sanctuary Tony and Renée occupied. "Looks as though the Taíno are going to be looking for a new God," was his final thought as his essence escaped.

Durius shook her head in disgust. "Chicken shit." A sword appeared in her hand, which she used to cleave his head cleanly from his body. She picked it up like it was a child's dirty laundry, calmly walked over to the fireplace, cleared the mantle with a brush of her arm, and placed the head dead center. "Whatever purpose Darius had in mind for those two will have to be modified." Durius lifted the edge of the sword to her mouth and licked off the blood. "Umm, tastes like chicken."

Barefoot, half-naked, and smelling like he never saw the inside of a shower, Sean ran full speed toward another half-naked man. The pointed stick in his left hand informed him of the purpose of his charge. The rush of adrenaline coursing through his blood blocked out any emotion, except his immediate survival instinct to survive.

Fortunately for caveman Sean, his stick penetrated the side of his opponent, dropping him to the ground where Sean repeatedly stabbed him with the blood spraying all over him until his victim stopped twitching. As Sean stared down on the bloody scene, his sanity returned for a split second before next finding himself a passenger standing in an Egyptian chariot in the middle of a thousand others. Instinctively he knew it was the Battle of Kadesh, Pharaoh Ramses II famous battle against the Hittites.

Billowing clouds of dust obscured the battlefield as the two forces violently collided, yet there was no escape from witnessing the gruesome slaughter in minutes of thousands of soldiers on both sides.

These visions of battle and his participation in them played out one after another so fast that all Sean could do was react to the threats in front of him. The rapidity of the action caused his adrenaline to boil over and the blood lust ran so high that even hacking down women and children became sport before it all ended.

This barrage on his senses continued all the way through to the battle of Gettysburg, where after he pulled his bayonet out of a Confederate soldier he realized it was one of his favorite cousins. Trembling, Sean dropped his rifle in panic and bent down to aid his victim. The Union forces had broken Picket's charge, so at least this time he didn't pay with his life for his act of vulnerability.

Sean sank to his knees and broke down. As he stared into his dead cousin's eyes, images of all of these past battles stared back at him. This attack on his savaged nerves would drive most humans into the embrace of insanity, but Sean calmly closed the dead soldier's eyes and in a daze stumbled to return to his place in line.

Without a second to focus his thoughts and with the memories of what he had experienced still raw in his brain, Sean once again returned to the cosmic path. Instead of the brutal reality of these past incarnations, this time a succession of movie screens that stretched throughout his childhood played out all around him.

From idealized renditions of family lives he could only imagine, to comedies and cartoons that allowed escape from reality, a sense of deep contentment washed over Sean. This continued through the adventures, whodunits, and fantasies, each one a reminder of how he used these to create his shield against his unhappy home life.

As he was about to surrender to the seductive pull these memories elicited, the abrupt introduction of shocking scenes he wasn't able to defend against slammed him. He shrunk back in terror as inhuman creatures ripped the flesh from screaming victims. Each scene came gift-wrapped with its own emotional terror similar to the layers of a cake stacked one on top of the other. No matter how hard he attempted to avert his eyes from the carnage or muffle his screams to hide how terrified he was, every drop of the sickness penetrated the core of his soul.

About the time Sean once again reached the limit of his ability to take it, the marquee on the Reseda Theatre announced the days offering, *Night of the Living Dead*. With a gathering sense of doom, he slowly walked down the aisle and took his seat to await the upcoming emotional onslaught. For the next fifteen minutes, he tried to hide his trepidation over what was to come. Then, as the lights in the theatre dimmed, a voice entered his head. "You know there is no one forcing you to torture yourself like this."

Sean remained defiant. "I can't let anyone know how weak I am. Everyone else can handle it, so I should be able to as well."

"At least until you can use the bathroom excuse to escape. I know all of your tricks, and guess what, so does everyone else. You fooled no one."

The memory of staring down at his dead cousin returned while he was in the Reseda Theatre in 1968. Sean sat up straight in his seat, looked over to the friends he grew up with, stood up, and walked out of the building without a glance back.

"Feels good doesn't it. Realizing you don't have to live your life at the pleasure of others."

In this, Sean realized another of his many contradictions. "So I joined the military?"

The voice pushed Sean to the limit of his existential awareness. "It was either that or politics. As I recall in one of the all-nighters we pulled at the whiskey, you were not going any other way. It didn't help when those Vietnamese flyboys showed up at our party with the arm candy."

This was a voice Sean both dreaded and welcomed as a long lost brother. "I thought you were the devil incarnate when all was said and done. I can't say I was surprised when you crashed and burned."

Carl's voice returned. "You moved on, so did I. Lost soul when I found him, lost soul when I left."

Sean closed his eyes and fondly remembered how their rapid-fire exchanges created a bond between them that years later still helped guide his actions. "Without Chris there would be no Tony or Alicia. My crazy would never have survived." He opened his eyes to find himself in the converted garage where the majority of his wildness occurred.

"You haven't couch danced since."

The same couch sat as a divider between the living room area and the bed, which they launched back and forth from while the New York Doll's *Trash* blasted at full volume.

Sean was tempted. "Only because the thought of seeing the couch-hopping Rear Admiral go viral on YouTube next to Tom Cruise wouldn't have gone over so well at the Pentagon." Sean smiled knowing in his private moments the punk still came out to play.

Sean's thoughts shifted. "Nice soft landing after that brutal montage you put me through."

"I'm not putting you through anything. Wherever you go is strictly on you. All I am doing is filling in the missing pieces along the way." When he finished speaking, Carl's voice abruptly disappeared to leave Sean alone once again.

— ❖ —

Tony took a bite out of the Tex-Mex burrito Renée magically made appear.

After she took a drink from her glass, Renée asked, "You know this can't turn out well for us don't you?"

Tony finished chewing and swallowed before he responded. "At this point all I want is a simple problem that I can either resolve with a brilliant tactical plan or punch unconscious. To go down fighting for something I understand sure beats sitting in this prison like a pussy."

For the first time since Renée returned, her emotions responded to his. "I'm not saying all is forgotten, but being with you again makes the waiting easier to take."

She started to reach over to him, when, without any warning, the force that held the streaming chaos at bay collapsed. Before they could comprehend what had happened, every atom in their bodies unzipped down to the molecular level and mixed into the flowing currents of colorful particles.

"There goes the anomaly." Aaron announced gleefully.

Durius turned and violently slapped her son across the face. "This is what got you in trouble the last time, you idiot. We have no idea if this is what your father wanted in the first place. Do you really believe he would leave such a vulnerability exposed for me to easily take advantage of?"

Used to his mother's vicious rebukes, Aaron meekly questioned, "Then why did you do it, and why didn't you do more damage than simply removing that pompous idiot's head?"

"Simply put, I don't care what your father thinks. I'm here, let him deal with it, and more importantly, I didn't want the rest of the Continuum to know I was there."

She then moved her face within inches of Aaron's. "As you know I have no right to interfere under the terms that settled our last little dust up, but that does not mean I lost the right of access to what was freely given."

Aaron quickly caught on. "So no one cares that you eliminated the guardian as long as you left everything else alone. Brilliant."

"Brilliant? There you go again. You lack the vision to see that nothing is ever lost or won in one event, no matter how overwhelming it may seem in the moment."

Durius paused to reflect before she continued. "Once these human creatures understood that by hitting someone over the head with a rock, and then stealing their woman and food was easier than hunting their own food, the idea stuck. That is the reason I loathe them. What fun is it to manipulate them when they are so predictable?"

Aaron couldn't resist another dig at his mother, damn the consequences. "And I always thought it was because fighting to get laid by the prom queen is what made them stupid."

Once again, to his surprise she only smiled. "I know of one prom queen's head that is going to end up on my mantle." Durius spent a moment to relish the thought before she gave her next orders to her son. "I have some important business to attend to, so while I am gone, stay put and let me know if anything starts to gain form."

"Whatever you say, *Mother*."

Once she was gone, Aaron smiled. "Yes indeed Mommy Dearest, it is a long game."

So tied up in their personal drama, neither Aaron nor Durius noticed the microscopic bonding of several cells that managed against all odds to hold their place in the streaming vortex, exactly in the same spot where Renée and Tony had vanished moments ago.

———————◦≡◦———————

A shower of explosions amid a number of brightly colored laser beams lit up the arena. With over 200 thousand wildly screaming fans demanding their star, he arrived in the middle of the fog-enshrouded stage gliding on a cloud. Without any musical back up, he broke into his first song.

Time takes a cigarette and puts it to your mouth.

You pull on your finger, then another finger, then your cigarette.

Before he could begin the next verse, the audience jumped the gun, and joined in, unfortunately lacking the knack for singing in unison.

You walk past the café, but you don't eat when you live to..."

"Cut, cut, and cut!" As the last cut escaped his lips, the stage, audience, and the arena melted away, which left Bowie alone in the middle of a barren landscape. "They can certainly take the time to create that perfect picture to post on Facebook, but can't keep a beat. The audiences who were there for the music ended somewhere in the 90s."

Bowie noticed Franklin had arrived. "How did you know to find me here?"

Then, upon a closer look at his companion, Bowie's attitude turned to concern. "What made you change your mind and come back? And why are you back to your lovable reptilian self? What went wrong?"

"Durius is what went wrong. The bitch hacked me up so bad I had to abandon the job before she started chewing on my bones. Oh, and how hard is it to follow the sound of your voice when you amp it up for an entire solar system to hear it."

"Just a private concert for a few of my closest friends." Without a word, the two shifted to a counter in a bar with two shots of whiskey and a beer back in front of them. "So were you able to find Darius and let him know?"

Franklin shot the whiskey and downed half of the beer before he answered. "I doubt anyone will be able to gain his attention for a while. I never figured he would take it so far for such a limited return."

Bowie laughed at his friend's assessment. "Oh, and you aren't hung up on Tony? This is where I differ from you and Darius. I know they are lovable at the individual level. Yet, when you put more than four of them together in the same room they become homicidal lemmings willing to jump off the nearest cliff when convinced of their moral righteousness."

Bowie did his shot with a beer back. The glasses refilled as soon as he put them back on the counter. "That, by the way, is why I chose not to invest."

Franklin gave Bowie an evil smile as he downed the second round. "So I suppose that means you are not ready to do that incredibly stupid thing we agreed to do?"

Instead of the drink, Bowie pulled a joint out of his pocket, lit it, and took a deep drag. "Like how we have spent the last 550 years wasn't already stupid? I am still trying to figure out how you let Darius rope us into his scheme."

Franklin laughed. "Me? Your ability to ignore the basic tenants of cause and effect never fails to amaze me. It must be truly wonderful to forget how he rescued our asses when we were stuck on that hellhole Fornata after you offended the entire race of Shirratins with your Robin Williams stand-up routine. I told you that would get us killed."

Bowie struck a diva pose. "An artist recognizes no boundaries."

"Anyway, we're moving on now."

The seriousness in Franklin's voice caught Bowie's attention, as serious wasn't a normal state of affairs between the two when alone together.

Franklin remained persistent. "You were there when he asked, and we both agreed."

"Au contraire, mon ami. I protested quite loudly before you caved. In case you haven't noticed, Mr. Oblivious, but not sticking our necks out is why we are still here. Out of the millions of years of them screwing with the life on this and the thousands of other planets we've visited, I can remember only a couple of hundred life forms that are still around. That is hundreds out of billions."

Franklin slammed down his drinks in disgust. "As long as we

don't piddle on the carpet or chew on their favorite shoes, yeah, we are nice pets to have around. But get in the middle of one of their family feuds and it's off with his head and put it on the mantle.

"I think it is time we stuck our necks out and tried something out of character."

Bowie's interest picked up. "So Captain Beefheart, what is your plan of action against one who can crush us like a cockroach?"

"I propose we both enter the deconstructed matter at exactly the same place we left Tony and Renée."

Bowie shook his head in disgust and powered down a full glass of whiskey. "If I come back half me and half god knows what, I am going to have to seriously reconsider our relationship."

In a rapid-fire motion, Franklin downed his whiskey and beer. "It's now or never."

Bowie raised his whiskey in salute. "In the immortal words of a certain preacher, *Son, we are on our own.*"

Flush with the excitement of taking his first bold move in a million years, Franklin wrapped both arms around Bowie. "Think about it. Two separate species separated by millions of years, who both carry the seeds of the Continuum, merged together. It will be magnificent."

As they appeared over the chaos, and then disappeared into, Bowie thought, "Yeah, like you haven't done anything this stupid before, you absentminded fool."

Surrounded by Rebecca's family brought about an uncomfortable disconnect for Alicia that Rebecca noticed. "Trust me, it will wear off."

"I don't see how. This world is as alien as can be to me. My eyes tell me the Statue of Liberty is standing where it should be and we flew over the Empire State Building, but everything, including your family is in conflict with the life I have shared with you in our home reality. How can they both exist?"

Sean Anthony interjected, "The same way two subatomic particles can be connected over light years of space. None of it is linear." Sean Anthony smiled at his wife who shook her head in a way that said, *here we go again.*

Alicia thought it best to get on solid ground, so she asked Phoenix, "How exactly does a woman wind up married to a demigod? Or have you two also done the same millennium dance as your in-laws?"

Alicia's comments stopped everyone cold. Phoenix decided a little fun might lighten the mood. "It all started when I fell for a simple farm boy who kept answering my requests with, *as you wish.*" Hell, he even fought off an evil prince after dying to reclaim our love." Phoenix maintained a straight face, as they all watched Alicia struggle with her explanation.

When the light bulb clicked, Alicia smiled and wagged her finger. "I do not think that word means what you think it does. *Princess Bride*, very funny. So the classics survived?"

Rebecca grabbed Alicia's arm and literally dragged her toward a nondescript three-story building across from the park. "Before we are totally lost in what is and what isn't anymore, let's get to the reason we are here."

When they reached the entrance, Sean Anthony took the lead and directed the group into an elevator that rapidly descended several floors.

When the doors opened to what the cavernous room held, Alicia struggled to maintain her calm. "These are the same patterns Sean disappeared into."

She then noticed in the swirling mass of colors a solid form rising up from the center. Something else in the scene didn't make sense. The patterns flowed like they came from somewhere else, yet Alicia's mind could not come to grips with how that could happen with four solid walls surrounding the surging currents.

Sean Anthony explained. "A little trick of spatial manipulation brought to us as a gift from Durius, though as of yet she doesn't realize it."

Rebecca seemed as surprised as Alicia was at what they were looking at. "Is this from the deconstructed reality, and what in the world is growing in it?"

"Sorry Mom. Events unfolded so fast, Dad thought it best not to explain too much. He needed all of us to act naturally within the situations we were directly involved with." Phoenix walked over to a door and opened it. Inside was a room almost as large as the one containing the deconstructed mass. "My part involved creating the containment field, which as you can see entails the expenditure of a tremendous amount of energy."

Rebecca understood much of the computer systems and mechanical equipment it supported, though there were some surprises. She knew the girl was smart, but... "I am impressed. There isn't any way on earth a system as complex as this could be built without my knowledge. What's the real story?"

Phoenix smiled at her mother-in-law. "We've been building it over the last ten years. Dad gave us a sample of the material in a small containment field, along with the story about what it represented."

Alicia turned her attention back to the containment field. Alicia couldn't get the image of the form growing out of the chaos out of her head. "Is that Sean?"

"No, it's Tony, Renée, and a couple of jokers you are familiar with."

Sean Anthony's statement was the final blow to Rebecca's pride. She grabbed her son by his coat lapel and shook him. "*Tony and Renée?* You told me they would be safe."

Alicia added her voice of dissent. "Is this from the same mess Sean disappeared into?"

Before Sean Anthony could begin to calm their fears, a hip looking man appeared from behind one of the rows of computers. Upon seeing the group, he stopped short and appeared confused. The sight of Rebecca altered his attitude. He walked out of the computer room and cautiously greeted her. "What's up Mrs. E?"

"You're involved in this too Adonis? Who didn't know, or was I the only one you felt it necessary to keep in the dark?"

That she had never seen Rebecca so angry before, in some strange way calmed Alicia. "For the moment can we please focus on what is going on in the other room?"

Sean Anthony jumped at the opportunity. "Sean is not in there and never was. None of this is actually here."

Sensing Rebecca's confusion, Phoenix interjected. "What you see here is not happening here."

Rebecca threw her hands in the air in frustration. "You guys built a trans-dimensional portal without letting me be a part of it? I am going to kill that husband of mine the next time I see him."

"Dad needed Sean with him somewhere else, needed you Alicia with Mom, and he needed Tony and Renée in the soup," Sean Anthony explained. "It all boils down to Dad needing Durius to believe Tony and Renée are more important than they are. And before you all fly into a tizzy about using them as bait, take a deep breath, we have it covered."

Sean Anthony pointed to the containment field. "*This* is one of the ways Dad intends to end the threat."

Rebecca was not convinced. "How does turning poor Tony and Renée into biological soup achieve anything?"

"First off Mother, it was the only way to integrate Franklin and Bowie's 250 million years of planetary life experience into Renée, and second, Dad wanted to flash a shiny bauble in front of Durius. Because of the changes he made to bring Renée back, she was the only one malleable enough. Adding Tony was purely an act of compassion." Sean Anthony waited for their response.

"So this all about creating some new super race?"

Phoenix answered Rebecca's question before Sean Anthony could. "Not a super race Mom, and if Dad could tell you what he did, he would have. All he wants to do is force the next evolution before Durius can end it all."

Bewildered, Alicia addressed Sean Anthony. "Though all of this is lost on me, none of it explains what Carl is doing with Sean." Then a light bulb went off, and Alicia raised her voice in anger. "Wait, are you telling me Carl is using Sean as his guinea pig?"

Before Sean Anthony could formulate an answer that would calm Alicia down, the energy levels in the room surged.

Adonis ran to one of the monitors. After a quick check, he warned, "Some serious shit is going down in the containment field."

⟡

At that moment, the guinea pig thought the same thing. As Carl disappeared, Sean's entire perception of the universe turned on its head. The sheer amount of traffic that passed through his consciousness made the I-405 Freeway in Los Angeles at rush hour seem empty by comparison, however, there wasn't anything remotely familiar about this. For all of the thousands of concepts about alien life and the structural makeup of the universe Sean had gleaned from a lifetime of reading, nothing prepared him for this novel assault on the core of his being.

A billion voices all talking at once and none of them listening filled every inch of his consciousness, while billions of watchers… "Watchers, where did that idea come from? Who's watching?" This paranoid realization disappeared as quickly as it came, replaced with a lifetime of actions taken and the countless justifications for taking them.

"You loved her. Why didn't you stay?"

"I was the best you ever had, and look how I turned out without you." Debra, 22 years old, gorgeous, rich, and always wanting to please. "You do want to be pleased, don't you?"

An audience to his own thoughts, Sean asked, "How can I grow if I am always taken care of? I need to struggle to evolve. Besides, how is she going to evolve if her life is all about me?"

"Will you look at that peacock? What an arrogant asshole. We were pulling that crap ten years ago." Sean is watching himself tearing Tony apart in his mind from the party where all of the up and coming Ensigns and upper brass mixed to sniff each other's asses. This was his first impression of his lifelong friend.

"Quick to judge this one." This was more of an alien thought that passed right through.

"There it is again." Sean wondered, "Is someone watching my thoughts?"

"His mind is a sieve. One look and you see all. Look at all that he hopes no one can access."

This intrusion was more violent. "Did another consciousness come in to rearrange my thoughts?" Sean wondered.

"Is everybody safely off the ship?" Sean watched as he lipped this concern to Tony as they stood on the Enterprise flight deck.

"Most have reached shore. All we have to do is trigger the command and she will be gone in minutes."

Their demeanor was solemn as they climbed down to the Admiral's launch. Twenty minutes later from a safe distance, they witnessed ten rapid-fire explosions tear through the massive aircraft carrier's keel. "Better at the bottom of the ocean, than try to change a reality we don't belong in."

Now old and frail, Sean watched in awe as he witnessed hundreds of thermonuclear detonations erupt, and feeling the blast rip through both his body and soul. Billions of screams rose to overwhelm his last terror. "So what?"

"This one tastes yummy." In horror, Sean's mind filled with the image of a consciousness he couldn't comprehend, violently penetrating Alicia using his body. Instead of horrified protest, which is what Sean expected from Alicia, he heard between gasps of pleasure, "What has come over you tiger?" More violent thrusting. "Don't you dare stop." The violent action drove them off the bed, and over the next ten minutes, they ingrained three different rooms with their excesses.

As soon as that mental torment ended, others took its place. "Look at how he fears his demise?"

"His awareness, or should I say the complete lack of awareness is stifling. I need to open some windows and let some fresh air in."

As the interloper raised the window, a stiff wind swept Sean into a rapidly moving stream of chaos that regardless of his valiant efforts to fight off fragmented his consciousness to the point he no longer retained his sense of identity. Instead, an awareness of every living thing he thought, dreamed, or at the time believed to be real erased his personal singularity. In this explosion of the fullness of all life in the tiny fragments that remained, Sean realized what the pot of gold he spent his entire life struggling to achieve represented.

Within this realization came an awareness of Sean's true reason for existence. "Represent an entire planet? Are you out of your mind? Einstein, Aristotle, Theodore Roosevelt, hell, even Eleanor Roosevelt makes more sense than a nobody like me. Everybody out!"

With all of the energy Sean could focus in his fractured state, he struggled to regain control over the marauding intruders. This only made matters worse as the release of his rage empowered the invaders to probe deeper.

Images of every moment Sean lost control of rational thought, everything from road rage over a stolen parking space, to being continually passed over for promotions by suck-ups who didn't know the difference between a Frigate and a Cruiser drove him deeper down the rabbit hole. "Look at how this rage mirrors how he goes about driving himself."

This same emotion manifested with Sean violently making love to another series of women, some because he sensed their need, others out of proving to himself that he could. Each scene came with its own critique. "Always needs to prove himself."

"Short life span, not much time for anything else."

"It started with his mother. Look at the pain the day he realized she despised him."

"How can a creature spend most of its existence trying to become something that is so hopelessly out of reach? Best to let them all go."

With each assessment, the rage grew, and as it did so did the violence of the images. Every fantasy he had of ending another's life that had started with his mother ramped up the indignities. In a series of Romanesque forums, armed with everything from a sword to an AK-47, Sean engaged in mortal combat with each one of those who had caused him unnecessary pain.

These violent confrontations changed to ones of verbal jousting as sadistic teachers whose heads literally blew up after a snappy jab of repartee aimed at exposing their failed dreams. "It's amazing that he would rather embarrass this one in a room full of his peers with facts, than cut off their head off with a sword."

Nighttime, deep into the Nevada dessert, car headlights illuminating a fat man laboring to dig what appears to be a grave. Three men with guns surrounded the terrified individual. "It's about time someone ended your lifetime of cons."

The face transformed into the corrupt building inspector with his hand outstretched. Then the childhood rival, who could never match Sean's skills, but used his social standing to impede him at every turn. Each time a new face, each time left not to die in a blaze of gunfire, but death by the searing heat after days lost in the desert without water.

"No guts to pull the trigger, even in his fantasies."

"Cowardly."

"Lacks intestinal fortitude."

"What a crybaby."

"What a crybaby? Really?" This fragment questioning his strength of will brought from deep within Sean's core a primal scream so loud in his head that every foreign voice went silent.

All at once, his mind returned to his control, which allowed the rest of Sean's fragmented thoughts to reform, though it took the last of his energy.

"Can you think of anyone better suited to such an important task?"

"What?"

As his vision cleared, Carl came into focus, at least it sounded like Carl, though from Sean's current perspective, this version of him consisted of pulsating streams of vaguely familiar colors.

"Seriously, I can't think of anyone else I would entrust with my wife's safety, oh wait a minute that is exactly what I did."

Then Sean could clearly see Commander Carl Eddington standing in front of him. "Service Dress Whites, really? I expected something a little more regal from you."

"After four years at West Point and over eighteen years in the Navy, what could be more regal than this?"

Sean had a million questions to ask his former subordinate, but one stood out from the rest. "What happened to the real Carl?"

"I am and have *always* been the real Carl Eddington, and as you also know, I served under you in one way or another since your first command." As he talked, a recognizable image began to form around them.

Back in the cabin of his first command, a much younger Carl sat across from him. "You were my second in command?"

"Correction – *am*. Do you remember our conversation?"

The memory was quick to return to Sean. "We were in the Gulf of Hormuz, and as I recall I ordered you to my cabin to go over the findings of your After Action Report."

Two shot glasses appeared on the table, which Carl poured Jack Daniels Single Barrel into and handed one to Sean. "That was when I knew you were the one. I was in command on the bridge when one of our F/A-18s splashed. We were under strict orders from CENTCOM [United States Central Command] to maintain strict station protocols while in Iranian claimed territorial waters."

Sean remembered that as the day Carl became part of his inner circle. "As I recall you disobeyed orders and went after the downed air crew and rescued them from rapidly approaching Iranian gunboats in direct disobedience of those orders."

Carl smiled as he recalled the event. "Yes, and the minute you were informed of the emergency, and my orders, you elected not to countermand me, and more importantly left my name out of the report as the one who ordered the violation. You took all of the heat, never mentioned it, and most importantly showed you didn't give a rat's ass about general orders when they posed an unnecessary risk to those under your command." As Carl finished, the room faded away and once again, they drifted in space.

"I imagine that spending an entire lifetime in the skin of a human must be exceedingly boring to one such as you."

Carl saw through Sean's attempt to learn more about exactly what he represented. "No different from any other experience, except one finds oneself having to suffer too many fools along the way."

The insanity of having a relaxed conversation drifting along in space finally became too ridiculous for Sean. "Seriously, as fascinating as it is to have my mind dissected by a million strange voices, where is all of this going?"

As Sean spoke, the space they occupied began to shift back into the same patterns of colors that appeared to go on forever. "You are now at the confluence of all of the life your consciousness can handle. Consider where you are as an on ramp speeding up to merge with traffic, but this highway never gridlocks. Are you ready?"

"You didn't answer my question." Then as they got closer to the maelstrom, Sean nervously asked, "Ready for what?"

Once again, Carl ignored his question.

As Sean moved to the center of his consciousness, his mind exploded into an awakening to rival that of a supernova. "So this is what it is like to experience God."

"Not quite, at least not by your narrow understanding of the concept. Instead, think of it as being able to access that 90 percent of the human brain that never gets to come out and play."

"He isn't kidding," Sean thought. Every memory in his lifetime flashed through in seconds, accompanied by thousands of images he hadn't noticed at the time. The people, the neighborhoods, and the structured chaos of everyday life took on new meanings. Instead of the casual acknowledgment and a quick discard that normally led to dead ends, they all now had clear paths backward and forward. "I see how they are all connected. How does anything work with so much of the picture inaccessible?"

"You were supposed to evolve into it, but unfortunately the allure of shiny baubles got in the way. All it took was a little manipulation here and a little manipulation there. Take for example how a man's little head always seems to win out over his big head, and you can understand why no one felt it safe to unleash your kind on the rest of the galaxy. You've been chosen to help end all of that."

Sean's mind rapidly strung together what this meant to him, and for that matter the rest of life on planet Earth. "Or die trying."

Without any warning, a bright flash of white light enveloped him.

"A little crowded in here, don't you think?"

"What did you expect, Franklin? In what alternate universe made you think this was a good idea?"

"Instead of whining about it, why don't you help me keep these two kids together? There is far too much ugly in this mess for me to do it alone."

Franklin was not exaggerating his need for Bowie's assistance. If the entire imagined or real aspect of life on planet Earth representing 27,000 years of history wasn't enough to sort through, then add in that none of it was coherent in its deconstructed state. Franklin and Bowie remained intact because their advanced DNA acted like oil to water in the maelstrom.

Using every trick learned over their 250 million years of evolution, they struggled to hold together against the raging energy of deconstructed matter. For a brief moment, Franklin lost his hold on

Tony against the surging tide, but a quick burst of energy supplied by Bowie gave them the strength to wrench the structures of Tony and Renée free and fully reform them within a small bubble.

In the cavernous containment room, the group watched as a shape began to ascend from the river of colors. At first, the shape mimicked the current it arose from, but then the familiar shape of Renée began to take form as it continued to rise above the swirling mass.

Everyone stared in amazement at what they were witnessing, everyone that is except Sean Anthony. He watched with a smile of satisfaction as the last remaining fragments reunited around Renée. A second form began to follow in the same spectacular fashion as Renée disappeared in a green mist.

The second shape revealed David Bowie, and as the costume he wore came into sharp relief, Sean Anthony had to clap in approval. He was clad in full shocking Ziggy mode, embellished by the star's seductively defiant pose in combination with the perfect androgynous makeup. Add the form-fitting tights he wore, stretched from one shoulder all the way down the opposite leg, which left little to the imagination on the other exposed thigh. He had a look that no one else in the world could have pulled off. He gave a quick wink in Sean Anthony's direction, and then he too was gone.

Before anyone could regain their equilibrium, another form in the familiar shape of Franklin emerged, bent deeply at the waist, smiled his crooked smile, and waved his hand in farewell before he too disappeared.

Sean Anthony shouted above the noise, "Shut the field down *now.*"

Adonis rushed back into the computer room to comply. Moments later the basement abruptly went quite as Adonis completed the shutdown. The massive room then shrunk down to the size of an average New York City tenement basement, complete with a row of highly irritating fluorescent light strips hanging from the ceiling.

Adonis had a grin that stretched from ear to ear. "I'll never get tired of this shit."

Alicia ratcheted up her sarcasm. "So, to all of you here who are in the know about what comes next, would you find it convenient to share with those of us still in the dark what the hell that was all about?"

When both she and Rebecca turned toward Sean Anthony and directed their glare at him, they were surprised to see he had noticeably relaxed.

"I can do better than that. I can show you."

Before they could question what he meant, green mist rapidly enveloped Alicia. "You better not be sending me to another place that hasn't invented toilet pa…" She vanished before she could finish.

⋅⋙⋘⋅

Renée had a saddle in her hands ready to throw onto the back of her horse, but the inescapable thought that she was forgetting something important stopped her. After struggling for several seconds to remember what it was, suddenly the damn burst and everything came rushing back. "How did I get back here?"

She dropped the saddle and ran to the house. She almost knocked Bowie down when she raced through the door. "Why am I back here and where is Tony?"

Instead of an answer, Bowie retrieved a joint from his pocket, lit it, and took a few quick hits before he offered it to Renée. Much to his surprise, she accepted the stick without hesitation and took a powerful hit. After two minutes of coughing her lungs out, she took another toke before she asked through the exhale, "Where is Tony?"

"Franklin is still working on it." Bowie answered concisely, as he thought he might reveal too much.

Frustrated, Renée lashed out. "Why did you stop? And no more half-assed answers. You lost the right to decide what I could and could not handle hundreds of years ago. And to this day, I still have no idea why you jokers left me stuck in the Twilight Zone for four hundred long and lonely years."

Renée reached to grab the roach out of Bowie's hand and almost fell over the couch in the attempt. "You do know I figured out what your game is a long time ago."

Bowie took a moment to enjoy the usually buttoned up woman lose a little of her self-control. "Can't keep anything from you." He retrieved what was left of his joint and took a long, satisfying drag before he offered it back to Renée. "Okay, even with you in this altered state, I wonder exactly what you think this game is that I am playing."

She took the offered joint, but instead of taking a puff, she waved it around dramatically. "You know the only other time I tried this, I became totally paranoid. Anyway, what you were saying?"

"Maybe you have had enough." Bowie tried to take the joint back, but Renée wasn't having it.

This brought about a round of silliness, punctuated by Renée playfully pushing Bowie so hard she knocked him right off his feet, her momentum enough to lose her balance and land on top of him.

As they lay tangled on the floor, it was Bowie oddly enough who realized they had better return to the matters at hand. "Someone needs a cup of coffee." After a lengthy struggle, he managed to pick her up and set her on the couch, as a steaming pot of coffee appeared on the table along with a cup, sugar, and cream.

An hour later, after Renée had emptied the pot and with her mask now firmly back in place, she demanded of Bowie, "Take me to Tony, or you better give me a damn good reason why you can't."

The coldness in her delivery made Bowie wish he had let her stay stoned. "It's really no big deal. Franklin thought we should send a message of our displeasure to her highness and took Tony with him."

Renée gave Bowie the *have you completely lost your mind* look. "Her highness? Who the hell are you rambling on about?"

Bowie realized he had waved a red towel in front of the bull. "Let me back up a bit. The most important thing for you to consider right now is everything is working out as planned. Take a moment to relax and simply accept that you are safe and Tony will join us as soon as he is able."

"*What*? I haven't relaxed since I found out that I used to be dead. Now where is Tony? And what the hell is going on?"

Bowie took a moment to decide if he should ignore her perfectly reasonable request. Then he thought, "What the hell, once more into the breach."

"Unfortunately, for you, as we are still in the middle of sorting out the details, it would be premature to offer what would only be conjecture at this point."

"Bullshit. You think I can't handle it, so you brought me back here to hide."

Bowie had enough. "You do realize that I am not the one who makes the decisions. Do you really believe that anyone would trust me to do anything remotely important? If you haven't guessed by now the one invested in what happens to you all is Franklin, not me. Speaking of Franklin, can you believe that sanctimonious bastard? As a matter of fact, he took me away from…"

"Can it Watson. I get it. I will have to wait for Sherlock to show up with Tony and…" Renée brought her face to within an inch of Bowie's to drive her point home. "And have *him* explain what the hell is really going on."

Renée wasn't sure if she still suffered from the effects of the potent weed, Bowie's laughable attempt at obfuscation, or that the last five hundred years of life had taught her everything was transitory. She took a deep breath and relaxed. "How long will it take before you know the outcome?"

Before Bowie could give her another non-answer, in a puff of green mist Franklin arrived in the proverbial nick of time. He held a bloody saber in one hand and in the other a severed head of a man. "It changes nothing, but we sure had fun."

Before Renée could react, Bowie stepped in. "This one asks too many questions, so if you would be so kind to explain yourself."

"First things first." Franklin disappeared, reappearing in Tony's Cuban home, where he strode over to the fireplace mantle to place Aaron's head next to his old one. With a quick nod of approval, he returned to Renée's home.

"Is somebody going to explain what's going on, or am I not supposed to question the severed head?" The absurdity made Renée state, "With some music, this could pass as one hell of an Off-Off-Broadway play that filled up with SoHo residents night after night. And why would I think of that? I know nothing about either Broadway or SoHo."

"I see what you mean, Bowie." A moist towel appeared in Franklin's hands that he used to scrub off the remnants of Aaron's blood. "However, to give credit where credit is due, she has intermingled with god only knows what, so it will take a bit to sort out everything she should not be feeling."

Bowie shook his head in agreement. "Still, you have to admit it is rather irritating, except when she gets stoned, then she can be fun to fool around with."

Renée decided she had enough of their act and walked toward the front door to go saddle her horse. When she opened it, she found the two of them standing in her way. "The head – Tony? *Now*."

Franklin's thrill of removing Aaron's head had subsided enough to consider Renée's confusion. "Tony is still with me, well me, and several million others of his lineage. It will take some time to separate it all out. Also, we cannot go back to your 2018 home reality, and no one dangerous can gain access to us here in the 1492 reality."

Now Renée was ready to explode. "If Tony is with you, why did you make him deaf, dumb, and invisible?"

Bowie slapped the back of Franklin's head. "You better have something better to offer than that. This woman is relentless."

"You needn't be so testy." Franklin was at first confused and then suspicious of what Bowie could have told her. Looking at Bowie, he inquired, "Relentless in what way?"

"All I'm saying is she expects some answers from you."

Renée fixed her piercing gaze on Franklin and furiously demanded, "If I don't find out what happened to Tony, and apparently me, in the next five minutes, someone else is going to lose their head."

Franklin nervously adjusted his wig before he turned on his charm. "One of the advantages that came out of reconstructing you is we were able to break down some of the walls that had previously prevented you from accessing certain talents."

Before Franklin could finish, a horrified Renée interrupted. "Reconstructed! You make me sound like a Lego set. What do you mean? What happened to necessitate reconstructing me? And *where the hell is Tony*?"

Bowie shook his head in disgust. "For someone who history has framed as a ladies' man, you sure suck at this."

Franklin frowned at Bowie before he answered Renée. "Listen girl. An evil entity snuck into this reality and managed to remove my head. I had to leave that body, which in turn caused me to lose control of your sanctuary. When it collapsed, the swirling mass of deconstructed material swallowed up both you and Tony."

Bowie pointed directly at Franklin and interjected, "The only thing you need to know right now is standing right in front of you. Say hello to your lover."

Renée looked first at Franklin, then back at Bowie and wondered which one to yell at first. Thankfully, once again five hundred years of experience with them had also taught her that if they wouldn't play nice, she wouldn't play at all. Besides, as usual, it was obvious they needed something from her.

Renée hadn't been stoned since high school, but that was nothing compared to her state an hour earlier. As she headed to the bedroom for a few hours of sleep, she commanded, "Wake me when you are ready to start making sense."

A relieved Bowie began to clap. "I really like this girl."

Renée was halfway through the bedroom door when Bowie announced, "Tony is here, because he is now a part of Franklin. It was the only way to hold him together."

Renée stopped, and without turning around, challenged Bowie. "Prove it."

"Ask to talk to Tony. Simply look at Franklin and say something as if he were Tony."

Renée slowly turned to face Franklin. The second she thought of Tony, there he was. She stared in shock at her former lover. "Every time I think it can't get any more bizarre, bam. The last thing I remember is we were in my house in that bubble surrounded by the deconstructed chaos."

"Also my last thoughts." Tony walked over and put his arms around her.

For all of her varied experiences over five hundred years of existence, Renée could not wrap her head around what was happening. "Have you been here all the time?"

"Think of it like sitting in the doctor's office waiting to be called. I'm not really a part of Franklin, only renting space." Tony waited as Renée tried to process the information.

"You know, it might be more helpful if I had another hit."

Tony could tell that Renée wasn't kidding and turned to face Bowie. "Really? You got her high?"

Bowie shrugged his shoulders. "Seemed like the right thing to do at the time."

Tired of waiting on the sidelines, Franklin returned. "Anyway, you were easier to fish out because of the changes that allowed for your longevity. While you and Bowie came here, I finished scooping up Tony. After waiting for him to quit bitching about becoming a part of me, I shared my unpleasant encounter with Durius and told him whom Aaron represented. I wanted to send a message of my displeasure back to her highness, and I thought it would be icing on the cake to have Tony along for the ride when I delivered it."

Renée held her hands out to stop Franklin. "Okay, back it up. The head? Aaron? Her highness? And who is Durius, and why are you saying her name like I should already know?"

"It turns out Aaron is Sean Anthony's brother from another mother," Tony quipped.

Now even more confused, Renée demanded, "Sean Anthony? Who the hell is Sean Anthony?"

Frustrated with Tony's interruptions, Franklin shoved him to the background. "As I was saying, Aaron is Durius' son by way of Darius."

"All of you just stop! Durius, Aaron, Sean Anthony, Darius, her highness, and you still haven't explained the head." Renée stopped to breathe.

Franklin tried again. "Darius is Carl, and…"

Renée erupted. "Now what the hell does Carl have to do with this? Carl as in Commander Carl Eddington? One of you better start making sense or you can kiss my ass goodbye."

Bowie and Franklin stared at her in stunned silence, before Franklin attempted once again to explain. "As I was saying, Darius is the one you know as Commander Carl Eddington, Rebecca's husband. Darius and Durius, the one I referred to as her highness, were former partners. Aaron Fletcher is their son, and the one whose head I cleaved. Sean Anthony is the son of Carl and Rebecca, and therefore, the half-brother of Aaron. All caught up with the who's who?" Franklin concluded.

Renée relaxed a bit. "Sort of, but continue."

"Now here is where it gets tricky. You see Darius and Durius are responsible for all life on planet Earth. Unfortunately for Durius,

Darius found his soul mate in Rebecca, which ended the partnership and turned Durius into the jilted, evil entity *ex* determined to destroy Rebecca and all of humanity in revenge."

Bowie could see that Renée could use some help, so he offered his joint. Without thinking, she grabbed it and took a hit. After another round of coughing, she replied, "So to sum it up, Darius and this Durius are responsible for all of this, and now Durius wants all of us dead?"

"Bravo!" Franklin clapped. "Fortunately for us, Durius was occupied somewhere else, which left Aaron alone and bored, and therefore inattentive to what I was up to. The second Tony was aboard, I invaded Aaron's space with *extreme prejudice*," Franklin finished with a flourish.

Tony flashed back in. "You sure went Buckaroo Bonsai with that sword for such a short and pudgy old man."

Feeling faint at the constant shifting of personalities, Renée dropped into the nearest overstuffed chair. "Could someone please get me a pop tart?"

Tony turned to comply, but Franklin returned in mid stride. "Though he isn't really dead, Aaron did have to leave to create another corporal identity. Besides, it all played out exactly as Darius had predicted."

"You mean he put us there as bait?" Renée showed less anger than she felt.

"He needed to keep her occupied for a while," Tony interjected, "and this was the easiest way to accomplish it. By the by, if you think you had it bad, Franklin gave up his head to sell it, and if you think that didn't hurt, I…"

Franklin took over again. "Your concern is touching my dear friend."

Then he replied to Renée's question. "You were in less danger than any of the other scenarios, and believe me the other options didn't have had any chance to succeed. Trust me when I tell you Durius holds all of the patents on your species' most horrific forms of torture.

"She had to believe she controlled events or she never would have bought it. As it is, if not for her bloodlust and obsession with Rebecca, she never would have believed Darius was that careless."

Franklin walked over to the bar, grabbed a bottle of wine, and opened it. "From here on out, you will be safe from Durius here. Besides, some friends of yours had a containment field around you the whole time, and they were keeping an eye on things."

It struck Renée that for all of the information that they had thrown at her, not one of their explanations gave her one bit of information about her place in it all. Thankfully for Franklin, Renée wasn't in any state to argue further. "Was it Rebecca?"

Franklin sipped his wine. "It's kind of complicated. She was there, but it was her son Sean Anthony and his wife Phoenix along with a master hacker named Adonis who performed the magic."

"What about Tony? When do I get him back?"

"If you wouldn't mind me leaving for a few days, I can bring him back as good as new," Franklin answered as he bowed low.

"Can you bring some KitKat's back with you?" Renée couldn't believe how wonderful that sounded.

"I'll do you one better." Bowie smiled as an assortment of candy, along with several bags from Taco Bell, appeared on the dining room table. "Stoners' delight."

The junk food went untouched, as that was Renée's last conscious thought for the next twelve hours.

⸻⋅◈⋅⸻

When the blinding light subsided, Sean stood in the crossing surrounded by the grandest Cathedral he had ever seen. Above the altar where the church usually mounted the suffering Christ on the cross, instead a marble statue of the Christian savior in the arms of a beautiful woman stood in its place. With childhood memories flooding his emotions, this contrary image of Christ made Sean laugh nervously, though through clenched lips, fearful of retribution from the priest he knew always lurked nearby.

"Come on. You can do better than that. Where you come from, there are many who would love to stone you to death for thinking of me having sex with my wife as normal. If only they could remember that whole *Son of Man* part."

Sean whipped around to see a man in his middle forties, who looked more like the Dude from The Big Lebowski, than the iconic historical figure sitting in the first pew of the nave. "I always imagined you looking thinner. It seems you haven't aged well over the last two thousand years."

"Not a problem." In a flash, The Dude morphed into the Jesus of popular myth. "Better? I mean, it isn't that difficult to play to your guilt ridden conscience. Carl thought you might be past all that by now."

Stung by the rebuke, Sean turned away and began to laugh at what had replaced the statue over the altar. This time fresh blood flowed from where the crown of thorns, nails, and sword wound penetrated the skin during the crucifixion. "No matter how many years knowing everything I was taught to be bullshit, I still get queasy in a church."

Jesus smiled knowingly. "That and the horrible wafers the priest gave at communion that stuck to the roof of your mouth. The richest cult in the world and still too cheap to pour a brother some real wine."

An open bottle of red wine and two glasses appeared on the wooden bench next to him. "Do you mind if I lose the robe? Wool is a bitch on my skin."

Sean looked up to see the sculpture had a Fender Stratocaster strapped on, tongue stuck out in rebellion. "Okay, so I am now in the presence of the Western world's greatest martyr. Where did Carl go, and why you? It certainly can't be because I've shown the ideal of you to be foremost in my mind."

"Faith is a bitch. Especially when those who profess to possess it in abundance are the ones most likely to be selling something you can't use." Jesus handed Sean one of the glasses of wine, and offered a toast. "Here is to believing what we can confirm, and acknowledging our ignorance of what we can't."

"Works for me." Sean clicked his glass and downed it in one go. Curious, he turned to see the statue in full combat gear, machine gun in hand, and a murderous scowl on his face. "So what gives with the CGI?"

"We are shifting from dimension to dimension, and you are witnessing the many different interpretations each dominate society chooses to represent me to those they subjugate. Yours happens to be near the top of the list onboard the guilt train. But then again, I always enjoyed spending my days with the riff raff of the lower wards than the spiritual posers who inhabit these phallic monuments. At least I could have a moderately entertaining debate about man's role in the greater scheme of things. That and science fiction conventions are always good for a hoot."

All of this fascinated Sean. "If such a person existed and possessed such a wealth of power, how did he allow his message to become as corrupt as those his message was meant to defeat?"

Jesus pondered the question before answering. "It all boils down to the greatest fallacy of them all."

"The idea of one superior omnipresent being of the male persuasion that sees and knows all?" Sean said this with all of the sarcasm he could muster.

"Nope. Yin and yang."

Sean laughed at the idea. "You know, I should have guessed that. I've come around to the idea that the way people view it is full of crap, which is another great way to explain humanity's gift of normalizing depravity."

"You can also put this at Carl's feet. Anything else you wish to be enlightened on?"

"So you are Carl's beard. You get all of the attention while he works behind the curtain."

Jesus downed his wine. "He did mention you were smarter than you looked. Carl has always been about the long game, so to answer the unasked question, yes, he put all of this into action thousands of years ago."

Sean reached for the bottle and filled both of their glasses. "From what I've seen so far, Carl can do whatever he wants without any regard to those he controls." He raised his glass for a toast. "Here's to guiltless gods."

"Amen to that bro."

Out of the corner of his eye, Sean could see the statue now posed in a dress and a bouquet of roses held at the front, like one of the transvestites Sean had witnessed cruising Castro Street in San Francisco. "Now there is a religion I bet it would be fun to be a member of," Sean sneered sarcastically.

Jesus threw his feet up on the prayer rail in front of him. "If I had the time I would show you how organized your kind can be when you let the queers run things."

Jesus then leaned close and in a whisper warned him, "You don't know the half of it. It isn't only Carl's ex who wants satisfaction. Think about all those who are offended by how he treated her. Unfortunately, almost every species that still couples, regardless of how advanced they claim to be, lose their minds when cast aside for next year's model."

"So I'm to gather all is not well from where you sit?"

Sean's deadpan response almost made Jesus fall out of the pew in laughter. "That all depends on how you define, well. When it comes down to it, from the minute Carl embarrassed his mate, your kind never had a chance. The plan all along called for another 100 thousand years for you to evolve into your big brain before the next step. More on all of that later; I am here for something entirely different."

"Sounds like the intro to the next mind fuck." The atmosphere in the musty old edifice began to weigh on Sean.

Jesus nodded in agreement. "I can't say I blame you for your current lack of enthusiasm. You drive yourself forward your entire life, always on your own terms looking for enlightenment, only to discover one day that your last original thought occurred over forty years in the rearview mirror. Now here you stand after having your mind and your identity stripped away, and then put back together. And here I sit, the image of your original disillusionment, boiling it all down to love and hate. That has gotta suck."

Sean was about to speak, but Jesus answered before Sean could ask, "Do any of the decisions and actions you have taken or are about to take make any difference? And how could they if those pulling the strings are every bit as screwed up as you? I doubt it, but if you didn't make the effort, I guarantee it."

Sean couldn't make up his mind if the words lit the bulb or the way Jesus spoke the words did. It didn't matter which, because for the first time in his life he felt all this sure beat rotting away in a cell after the Navy arrested him and Alicia in 2014.

A smile spread across his face. All at once, he realized that everything since the Enterprise Task Force deployed out of San Diego back in 2014 put him front and center in the battle he had yearned for all of his life. "All or nothing; end it for good," went through the imagination of the 4-year-old stay at home kid that still resided in his memories. "How many people have you and others such as Carl given this much responsibility to?"

Jesus scratched the stubble on his face, before he answered. "Well, once again that all depends on what we have given you. For example, Rebecca has more scientific knowledge in one of her fingernails than you, and I am confident no one will turn to you to engineer a viaduct. Besides, them ain't part of the rules where you're concerned."

"What rules?" Sean wasn't sure he wanted to know.

Jesus ignored the question. "There are too many life forms to mention, but suffice it to say the way any species evolves is to come into contact with others, usually much older ones like me, who can strip away their mountain of contradictions. Unfortunately for your particularly brutal species, the obsessive manner in which you strive to annihilate every living thing you encounter complicates things. As I stated earlier, you were not supposed to be ready for another 100 thousand years, minimum, yet with Durius making it her mission to eradicate you from existence, adjustments had to be made." Jesus morphed into Siddhartha Gautama, the Buddha, and yes, he smiled.

"Durius?"

"Who do you think I have been warning you about? Durius is Darius' former mate, and in a short while the one you will have to deal with."

"Durius, Darius? You have neglected to explain who these two are."

Darius is who you know as Carl, Durius is the woman he spited to hook up with Rebecca. Try to keep up."

"This is all about a love triangle?"

"Not really. It is hard to explain to someone with, shall we say a limited ability to understand." Jesus knew that to explain further would make what was to happen next more difficult for Sean to survive.

"That's it? And exactly how do you propose that a middle-aged nobody, who couldn't change the ethics of an organization that ironically made every new member swear an oath that none of their superiors lived by, accomplish this?"

Instead of either Jesus or Buddha, Carl now stood next to Sean outside of a thatched hut in the Irish countryside that looked right out of the movie *The Quiet Man*. "That you demand so much from yourself as an example to others is how. You have already taken the first steps."

———

Franklin smiled as he admired the heads on the fireplace mantle at Tony's house in Cuba. Lying on the couch was a small boy of about

10 years old, who by the look on his face was not a happy camper. "Why the hell am I a kid, and better yet, why am I naked?" He scrambled to wrap the couch cover around his body.

A mirror appeared in Franklin's hand, which he handed to the child. "Sorry, but it could not be helped."

The boy grabbed the mirror and after a quick glance jumped up off the couch. "How did this happen? Did you do this to me?" Tony stared in amazement at the length of his hair that grew as he looked at it.

"Relax Anthony. You will be good as new in a couple of days." With a towel and a pair of scissors in his hands, Franklin placed himself behind Tony. Then, with the flourish of a conductor, he began to cut large swaths of hair from Tony's scalp.

"The last thing I remember is falling and trying to grab Renée, but she was gone. Then…" Tony paused in shock. "Wait a minute!" Tony whipped his head around to face Franklin, who fortunately had prepared for such a sudden move and withdrew the scissors before they could slash the side of Tony's head. "How could you put me back together inside your body?"

"Well, yours truly, with a helping hand from Bowie, jumped in after you. We then found pieces big enough to put both you and Renée back together again. All I can say is in the annals of human history there has never been recorded a more selfless act than the one Mr. Bowie and I performed."

Tony didn't hear a word Franklin said. "I remember fragments of other lives, and the strange thing was they were not only fragments of people. I could communicate with everything from spiders to trees, and weirder still, empathize with them. How can you empathize with a tree?" Tony stopped when it occurred to him that Franklin stood there with the same old eyes above the glasses that said, *But of course you can.*

Tony rebelled at the idea. "If it was one big dream, there is no way I would remember all of it." Then another realization struck

Tony. "And *exactly* where is Renée right now?" When he saw the look on Franklin's face, he jumped off the couch and demanded, "You better tell me she is all right, and that there is a good reason she isn't here."

"What part do you want first?" Franklin calmly motioned for Tony to sit back on the couch and let him finish cutting his hair.

"Go straight to the part about where she is."

Once again, Franklin motioned for Tony to comply, which he did knowing damn well he wouldn't get anywhere if he didn't.

"Relax tiger; she is at her home in Wyoming."

"So if she is at home in our 1492 reality, who do you have making sure…?" Tony again jumped up to face Franklin. "Tell me it isn't Bowie keeping her safe."

"Okay, I won't. Instead, I could try to explain to you, a creature that has only been conscious for less than one ten thousandth as long as I, what it was you experienced as trillions of atoms. And let's not forget how long the real ring leaders of this circus have been around."

Tony threw his hands up in surrender and took a moment to decide which one of his current predicaments was the most important to rage about. "Maybe you could start by explaining to me how long it is going to take to bring me back to my mid-forties."

"If you mean your late forties, I don't know. I've never done this before. Now can I return to cutting your hair before it takes over this room?"

So engrossed in the conversation, Tony hadn't noticed his hair nearly reached his feet.

Another change rapidly approaching was puberty, which Franklin realized was not going to help matters. "My guess would be soon based on that mountain of hair."

Tony reluctantly took his place on the couch, and Franklin made short work of whacking him down to the scalp.

"How exactly did you put me back together?"

"You would be better advised to understand how your former girlfriend thinks and what motivates her and leave it at that."

"Not good enough old man. Spill."

Franklin walked around the couch to sit in a chair facing Tony and placed his hand on Tony's knee. "Probably because the only way I could bring you both back was to add a little something special to the mix, and this little something was me. In Renée's case, Bowie did most of the work, which says something about her inner fortitude that she managed to maintain her identity intact. Fortunately, when we brought her back, she wasn't able to keep those memories. Could you imagine the added chaos that would have brought to the poor child?"

"As entertaining as this has all been for you, if you didn't think Sean and Alicia have much of a chance to succeed, why are you still sticking around? How could everything you've put us through be a lost cause?" The words spilled out of Tony's mouth without thought. "I have no idea where that came from."

Then he accused Franklin of a monumental betrayal of trust. "You've been in my head all along, and Renée's too?" Tony pushed Franklin's hand away and stood up only to experience excruciating pain from his head to his toes, which caused him to collapse to the floor.

Speechless, Franklin slapped his forehead hard in punishment for not thinking that some of his thoughts would make their way into Tony's consciousness. "I'm sorry I forgot to mention the bit about how painful growing up at the accelerated pace is going to be. Concerning whether or not I have any faith in the ability of your friends to save your species, it is irrelevant to their success."

"And the ability to invade my mind is still okay with you?"

"Though it would be fruitless to deny I have the ability to access your thoughts, I have not. If your concern is a lack of free will on your part, at no time did I or anyone else manipulate you in any way to make decisions contrary to your own wishes. You have always maintained freedom of choice."

Tony then entered Franklin's thoughts. "I can clearly see this is mostly a game to you, however, apparently against your better judgment, you do care."

Franklin gently pushed Tony out of his thoughts, but not before Tony took a peak behind his alien curtain. "Man, this guy is old. And he and Bowie are dinosaurs?"

Conflicted about how much more he should reveal, Franklin manifested an ancient earthenware jar of wine, only this time instead of being open and ready to pour, its stopper remained sealed. "You know I have carried this with me for the last two thousand years. It was a gift from a special friend. He put it aside for me when he celebrated his last supper before he went out in a blaze of glory. I think it fitting that we should share it today, however, morally speaking getting your now 15-year-old ass drunk would be considered child abuse to your uptight generation."

Without another word, the stopper blew off, and two ancient ornate wine goblets appeared on the table. "Bowie got these from Cleopatra after a well-earned night of carnal pleasure."

Tony experienced another round of shooting pains. "Damn that hurts. Okay, you are rambling to avoid answering my question. Really, how bad is it?"

"Here, drink this, but before you do, could you please try to remember there isn't any way for me to condense a quarter billion years of life into words that will ease your concerns." Franklin handed Tony a goblet and held up his to toast. "Here is to your living another million years to have all of the answers you desire."

After they downed the drinks, Franklin put his hand back on Tony's leg. "I have known Darius for a long time, and believe me when I tell you that I may not always agree with his choices, but he is committed to keeping you and your species alive. Even with all of the violence and carnage your species has wrought over the years, he always believed you would eventually evolve toward something more elegant. Unfortunately, Durius has made that impossible, ergo where we stand now is win big or be ground to dust."

Franklin paused as he replaced the wine bottle and goblets with shot glasses and a bottle of Mortlach 75 Years Old Scotch. After he poured and they downed, Franklin unwisely added, "Then of course when you factor in that Durius allowed outsiders to add their presence to the proceedings, the demand for epic scenes of destruction escalated accordingly."

"So you're telling me one of the reasons for all of the suffering is to entertain out of town guests?" Tony realized that would explain much.

"Why else do you think you were gifted with the hydrogen bomb? Bow and arrow leads to muskets, which leads to cannons, to missiles, and on. When the carnage brought about by the First World War became too predictable, boom, an additional 20 million dead in the Influenza epidemic of 1919. WWII, the Cold War, followed by endless war around the globe, yet here you still are.

"Anyway, this is why the intensity needed to be continually ratcheted up to the point of Armageddon. Though Durius spent most of her time trying to end your world when Darius first went native with Rebecca, she could not overcome the spectacle that so many off world species came to count on. Well that, and Darius' constant mediation to make sure they would keep coming to the show."

"Like I said, we kill each other to entertain out-of-towners." Tony poured another round, which after a click of shot glasses they downed.

Franklin continued. "Let's face it, Darius, Durius, the one you call Jesus, and three you haven't met yet infused you with their DNA, and half of those did so for that express purpose. There had to be elements that counterbalanced. For example, love and lost love, hate, artistic creativity, sadistic oppression, the endless curiosity to create, and the never-ending desire to destroy. Why do you think you are constantly bouncing irrationally from one to the other, and sometimes all at the same time? That makes it difficult to foresee the outcome, consequently increasing the mayhem. You would be absolutely disgusted to discover most of the species in the galaxy still get off on the things they themselves evolved beyond. It's similar to watching monkeys at the zoo throw shit at people."

This time Franklin poured the shots. "Here's to all of the monkeys and their handfuls of shit."

Maybe it came from a part of Franklin still buried deep in him, or maybe the shock to his now 20-year-old system had subsided, but Tony thought he could see part of the bigger picture come together. "My guess is some are worried that we humans might be able to jump up to a level where we could threaten this quaint little spectacle."

"Well, yes and no. I will let you in on a little secret. The reason they left us dinosaurs alone for as long as they did was that they lost interest. All of the action lately has been a conflict over one hundred light years away from Earth that made the Star Wars planet killer a mere speck of dust in comparison. When that ended, retro became the fad. Primates were in and we were out, because, frankly speaking, we were boring to watch. We ate, we shit, we slept, we occasionally fought, and we died, not enough chaos to meet their needs. Simple treks across the landscape in search of food don't draw the best of ratings."

Tony felt the bitterness behind Franklin's words.

Franklin further explained, "Then after millions of years, as a thank you for leaving the planet in excellent condition, Bowie and I became as we are. They packaged a complete history of dinosaur evolution neatly into our two small nobodies. It is nice to keep some pets alive in case they want us to make a comeback. Since then we have had 62 million years to figure out, with Darius' assistance, how to fit into our current niche. We are a part of this for precisely that reason."

This time Tony poured the shots and promptly downed his. "On one hand, you speak of a cosmic battle that raged for eons that I assume ended badly for one side of the combatants. Yet apparently, they didn't pose a risk, but little old monkeys like us do? That doesn't make any sense."

Franklin downed his shot. "It does when you consider that merely possessing the ability to kill and destroy in all of its gruesome glory, doesn't compare with the analytical attributes that they gifted to your species. Darius and others realized from that interstellar spat that they needed to add an element of personal risk to raise the stakes. Another truth for you to wrap your head around is neither of those warring factions survived, except for only one from each side. The last I checked those two spend most of their time torturing small animals on an obscure speck of a planet in an obscure corner of the galaxy. But that is a story for another day."

"So that explains motive, but still leaves out that the only thing left to do is have us go out in a huge final Big Bang, which…" Tony paused, confused about why it was so difficult to form a clear thought. Then it hit him. Accelerated metabolism, three shots of Scotch, and two glasses of wine equal hammered time.

Franklin didn't try to hide his amusement.

With a glare in his direction, Tony gamely soldiered on. "The ending everyone expected certainly didn't happen. Hell, any writer worth his salt could have produced a series of blockbusters that would have squeezed out at least another one hundred years of brutality before we cratered."

"Well, then there is Durius, and that my dear boy is the only reason why we still have a chance. Because of her unbridled hatred of Rebecca, she is liable to break the rules. That would allow Darius, to challenge her actions and ask the Continuum to revoke her access to all of Earth's realities. A judgment in his favor will allow Darius to complete his plan without her interference. Besides, everyone enjoys the drama of a domestic spat to liven up the day.

"On the bright side, if Sean manages to survive, and if all of the other pieces in play succeed, a new and improved humanity can inhabit your world in a new paradise. Sound like fun?"

"Then why are you so worried? Could it be that you believe Durius is well prepared for what Carl is trying to do?"

"How much did Tony see while a part of me?" Franklin thought. "It is all for naught if she manages to kill off the six of you. Since Carl is with Sean and Alicia, Rebecca is with Sean Anthony, Jesus is keeping Osaka safe, and Bowie and I saved you and Renée, she might let things proceed without further hostility."

Tony didn't see it that way. "Pigs will fly and the Sun will rise in the west. It seems to me from a personal perspective that she already succeeded in killing us once, so what's to prevent her from doing it again?"

Franklin's demeanor became menacing, which revealed the true nature that lay at the center of his being. "I most certainly hope she tries."

Rebecca stared at where her friend had stood for a moment before she tore into her son. "You better start explaining what your father is up to, or so help me, you will discover you are never too old for me to make you cry like a little baby."

Sean Anthony put his hands up in surrender. "Relax Mom. I guarantee you that Alicia will be pleased with her destination."

"So you created all of this to open a portal into our home world?"

"From a purely technical perspective, you would be wrong." Sean Anthony continued before his mother could object. "It isn't a portal in the strictest sense in that we are not connecting to points within the same dimension."

"As I was about to say *before you interrupted me*, it is how you and Carl travel from one dimension to the other. The only difference with this set up is you can move people and material."

Sean Anthony should have known better than to think his explanation would do anything but inflame her anger. However, instead of offering a quick mea culpa, he made matters worse. "With so much on your plate because of your personal connections, Dad thought we could handle this on our own."

"So because I'm a woman you mean, and because I am a woman I wouldn't be able to separate my emotions from what needed to be done. I suppose next you're going to suggest that I should go home and make sure dinner is on the table by six."

"Awkward." Adonis broke the stunned silence in the room.

After throwing him a nasty glare, Phoenix punched him in the shoulder. "Believe me Mom, we thought we were helping. If we had any idea this was how you would react, I never would have agreed to leave you out of it."

Rebecca wasn't convinced. "Yes indeed. Why wouldn't you want to have one of this world's leading scientists involved with one of the most technological experiments in history on the sidelines?"

Sean Anthony tried again. "I am truly sorry Mom. Dad thought that after all you have been through, you should have the time to enjoy your family?"

Everyone waited silently to see if his explanation would placate Rebecca. They didn't have to wait long. "Fine. So what else have you kept from me, or better yet what happens next?"

To keep Phoenix from punching him again, Adonis moved out her range before he spoke. "Don't you want to know how long it took us to pull this off?"

Phoenix glared at Adonis before she used everything she could think of to calm Rebecca down. "Better yet, why don't we focus on all of the wonderful changes that have occurred since we began? After all, it did consume the better part of the last thirty years to do it. Then there is your granddaughter."

Her last comment hit home. Rebecca's anger morphed into a smile. "I can't believe how much you have matured since the last time we were together, but then again, you are the parent of a teenage girl."

Rebecca then took a long hard look at Sean Anthony. "So let me get this straight. Out of the over seven billion people from the reality Adonis and I came from, all but Sean and Alicia, and those in the Enterprise Task Force are all that weren't swallowed up in that biological goo you pulled Renée and Tony out of?"

"In strictly human terms, from the 2018 home reality, only seven remain; Sean, Alicia, Tony, Renée, Daniel Osaka, Adonis, and you, Mom. Dad used the same interdimensional bridge he constructed to send you all back to both 1942 and 1492 to return the task force back to 2018 after the Grey's disruption."

Rebecca looked shocked at her son's emotionless explanation. "Why would he do that?"

Sean Anthony knew he couldn't lie to his mother. "Because to continue keeping matter that didn't belong to a given reality in place would have kept Dad from achieving the final solution."

"That sounds a little too close to what a madman we dealt with in 1942 tried to do." Rebecca then realized another issue with her son's explanation. "What about us being here? Are you saying we can't remain in this place where we built a better world, a world that we have kids born into?"

Before Sean Anthony could reassure her that it wasn't as bad as it sounded, his head jerked up. "We have a problem."

Phoenix felt it as well. "Looks like we have company."

"So what was with the spiritual idols bit?"

"Cromulus is a friend of mine. You might call it a vetting process. The Buddha was his idea, after all he represented a kinder, gentler God, and one he thought was closer to the manner in which you live your life, similar to your fantasy of living in a home like this one."

Sean laughed. "Right, *The Quiet Man* movie. Only my Maureen O'Hara would be Alicia, and I'm closer to resembling Andy Griffith than John Wayne. That would be Tony."

Carl motioned for Sean to follow him to the front door of the Irish cottage. "Of all the characters you have represented over the last ten thousand years, who you are right now is a perfect representative of all that mankind should strive to be."

"Well isn't that a sorry testament to how far we have declined as a species." Self-importance was never an issue for Sean.

"Not surprising that you would need convincing. It's no wonder you find it so difficult to judge yourself fairly when the majority of your heroes also happened to be their own best press agents."

"Come again?"

"You see a stoical genius when you think of Thomas Jefferson, years ahead of his time. Biologist, farmer, intellect, author, inventor, a man with an unquenchable thirst for knowledge, oh and author of one of the most important documents ever written."

"And the problem with that is?"

"The problem is how you excuse his hypocrisy. You could start with equal rights for all men, but not women nor his slaves. Then there is his political yellow journalism attacks that would make the people at Fox News too nervous to air. Not to mention his total lack of loyalty to anything or anyone that got in the way of his political ambitions.

"Though you carry many of these thoughts, the difference is you could never justify the contradictions to be able to act on them. You're a goddamn saint by comparison."

Sean rose to his hero's defense. "Whether or not his positives outweighed his negatives you can't escape that he helped change the world, and no one outside of Franklin did more to push a deeper understanding of our world into the average person's awareness. There is a reason they called it the Age of Reason."

Carl countered. "Voltaire yes, Jefferson no. Trust me, as every aspect of that revolution flowed through me. Who do you think advised Washington to show up in uniform in front of the Continental Congress, and who had him resign his commission and return home after the war? For every Jefferson, there came a

Hamilton to conflict with a Burr. Lincoln, Douglas. Before them, Nelson had De Grasse, Napoleon, Lord Ellington, and on and on. The message never changed, only the players in the game. Anyway, the point I am trying to make is I have seen into all of the dark corners of your mind, and the worst I could find the Academy of Motion Picture Arts and Sciences would rate PG. Like me, you are a hopeless romantic."

All of this made Sean extremely self-conscious. "I'm a romantic because I want the world to work the way it should? It doesn't matter if everything you say is true, isn't it a sad state of affairs that there aren't enough who feel the same way to make a difference?"

"And there it is. Just because you have been looking in the wrong places, doesn't mean they are not out there."

Once again Carl and the cottage faded away, this time replaced by a rundown kitchen where a young man in his mid-twenties sat at the table with his head in his hands. The distant sound of a baby crying and her mother's calming words barely penetrated his consciousness. "Will it ever stop being so hard," replayed in a loop. "I had a chance to get out of this hellhole, yet..."

"Honey, could you please run down to the store. I have one diaper left and this morning's applesauce is not agreeing with your little princess."

One look into her eyes ended his bout with self-pity. As smart as he thought of himself, his intellect paled in comparison to the mother of this child. Two days after she discovered her pregnancy, the University of Texas had offered her what for a hardscrabble scrap of a town like theirs was the Golden Ticket out. Without complaint, or regret, Casey rejected the scholarship, and accepted her new responsibility. "Maybe someday our daughter will be the one."

Small intimate stories of the common clay played out for what to Sean felt like weeks. No matter the adversities, the injustices, or outright tragedies, each event drove home the same point, an entire network of people existed who carried the same dream, and regardless of circumstance never stopped believing. The other striking similarity to these stories displayed an unerring belief in the long game.

From every culture came examples of these politically weak, oppressed, and disenfranchised individuals passing down this inner strength to their children. Over the course of the following generations, this staying power of stability produced wealth and prosperity that ironically then created a new batch of entitled little sociopaths who were every bit as oppressive as their forebears were. Shiny baubles won out more often than not over the discipline necessary for the long game their parents had sacrificed for.

Even with all of this evidence to show the tremendous lack of foresight inherent in humanity, the fallow seed of the long game remained as the cycle repeated.

A bitter chill swept through Sean when all of a sudden a thousand alien ideas ripped through his brain at once. Visions of worlds he never imagined, complete with the lives of the aliens who traversed the surfaces flooded his consciousness. In one particularly vivid scene among the many, a biped similar to a human, however, this one included black wings folded to his side that contrasted with its light brown skin stood stoically staring off into space. Standing off to the side was one with wings of white.

The black-winged one rubbed its beak lovingly on the nap of the other's neck before it unfolded the most beautifully colored wings Sean could imagine. Then, with a mighty leap, it became airborne. Though fascinated by the display of affection between the creatures, it wasn't until Sean shared the rapidly ascending creature's consciousness that he realized it was off to his version of work. The birdman's mind filled with the mundane nature of the day that he knew was in store.

Throughout the thousands of alien images that followed, the common thread among the majority was the repetitious nature of their lives.

Entering into the periphery of his thoughts, Carl advised Sean, "It doesn't matter how long your species or you live, there is always certainty in the mundane nature of all life. All that you lack is the perspective that comes from interacting with the millions of those who experience millions of years as normal. Death is something that happens to stars and planets, not them."

Carl continued. "To bring the analogy down to earth, try to imagine what it would be if you spent a thousand years in that rundown kitchen with limited human interaction. That is a metaphor of the last ten thousand years of your existence. Humanity never had the chance to leave the safety of your home because thanks to Durius' meddling, the Continuum decided you were much too dangerous as currently constituted."

Before Sean could respond, the scene shifted once again, creating another memory overload. Though the images at first glance appeared familiar, a subtle shift began to take place as a shroud lifted off the people and places his life had crossed paths with. This time alien shapes marched through. With the exception of the classical renderings of the Greys who always emitted a sense of menace, the similarities of these alien creatures outnumbered the differences.

The biggest shock came when Sean's view shifted skyward to discover alien craft of all sizes and shapes traveling over a planet devoid of human civilization. When he returned to the present, he and Carl stood in a beautiful garden paradise. "How long ago?"

"When the decision came to end the age of dinosaurs over sixty million years ago, Earth became what you would refer to as a vacation spot for those of us who wanted a quiet out of the way spot to relax." Carl picked a rose from the garden, and handed it to Sean. "Most of the current flora we imported from other planets in the galaxy, and most varieties are as robust in their complexity as you."

Sean blinked once and now stood in the shadows of the world's tallest trees, the California Redwood or *Sempirvirens Gigantia*. Based on the vast numbers of giants, he guessed this was a time before man figured out how to eradicate them to near extinction. Before he could ask Carl why here, the ground beneath him came alive. From the tree nearest, a giant spider web network of pulses intersected with the other trees, which in turn had their own signals pulsing outward. The entire forest floor resembled the graphics of a modern computer network.

"The network under your feet is a thousand times more complex than anything man could solder together, and that is without adding what is going on above." Carl pointed out the explosion of chemicals that erupted from the millions of needles in the forest canopy. "Each one of those colors represents different chemicals, some of which repel predators, others that welcome symbiotic relationships. The power to heal, the ability to send out warnings of danger for hundreds of miles, emotions that feel loss and pain, and hundreds of other defined senses that humanity had never considered in their ignorant race to exploit. This forest covers an area of three thousand square miles and interconnected in a way only a select few of your kind could understand."

Overwhelmed by the incredible beauty of these gentle giants, Sean had barely heard Carl's words. "How could we be so deaf and dumb?"

"Purely by choice. You had people such as John Muir try to show you, but how do you convince a species so wrapped up in their momentary pleasures to take the time to understand their true cruelty. Everything on this planet was interconnected until humanity's savagery hacked it to bits without a second thought." Carl went silent, and as he did, he released his own chemical signal that reached out and intermingled with the trees, which brought a satisfied smile to his face.

Once again, as the power of the forest around him overwhelmed his emotions, Sean remembered how it felt to be part of something so much bigger than himself. "I understand why we spend so much of our lives lost. We can't see the forest for the trees."

Carl groaned at Sean's pun. "Why do you think your existence is at stake? Regardless of her personal grudge, Durius isn't wrong to want your kind eradicated. Humanity is one of the most one-dimensional species ever created, and the reason you lasted this long was the entertainment your barbarism brought to those who watched. It is also the reason so many visit Earth. There are few other places in the galaxy that act so incomprehensibly."

"So why try so hard to save us?" Carl's earlier explanation had further confused Sean. "I can buy most of that, except the part where you placed us in the middle of two of the most brutal periods of human existence and our only options were more of the same. There wasn't too much empathy involved when we took out the Axis leadership in WWII or reordered the power structure of 15th Century Europe. We did both at the end of a gun."

Carl shrugged his shoulders. "Though I knew neither situation was ideal, each showed your first instincts were to consider the impact of your decisions before you acted, and in both cases you strove to create a more just world. Never did you, Alicia, Tony, Renée, Rebecca, or Daniel consider taking the easy way out, or place yourselves in situation for personal gain. You all wanted something greater."

As Carl answered, the forest shifted back to the Irish cottage, however, this time Alicia stood at the front door. Carl motioned for Sean to go to her. "We have some time, so enjoy it while you can."

Sean watched as Carl faded away in a green mist before he walked over to his lover. "So how was your day?"

<hr/>

Durius stood on a promontory that overlooked the latest changes to a planet only she possessed the authority to change at will. An exact mirror of San Francisco spread out across the vista below. She had created this version of the city with all of its biological inhabitants purely for her amusement.

Durius was beside herself as she thought about how Cromulus had manipulated her into that horrible agreement. "Why did I agree to stay away from both Rebecca and Sean Anthony, and who has the right to judge me if I decide to interject myself across realities or not?

"First, two parasitical creatures move across dimensions in a blatant attempt to circumvent protocols, and then they impart our advanced awareness into their empty heads."

Her voice of dissent replied. "Since when would I challenge another's interpretation of creation? Besides, I am only upset because of his dalliance with that human bitch. Maybe I should have let it run its course."

This split personality self-judgment surprised and enraged Durius. "Am I judging my reaction to his outright betrayal as if my anger doesn't matter?"

As Durius fumed, she absentmindedly opened up a portal to see Sean tenderly kissing Alicia. "Then there is this. Here I stand in judgment of myself while this primate commands the attention of those a thousand times his equal. Since when did insanity become the order of the day?"

Disgusted by the sight of the two primates sharing their affections, Durius violently closed the portal. After she took a moment to decide what her next action would be, a smile spread across her face. "Since when do I need permission from anybody?"

She then moved to the middle of her version of downtown San Francisco. Though all of the male characters that wandered around her had their own distinctive identities, the same was not true for the women, both young and old. She grabbed the nearest one by the throat and slowly squeezed the life out of the horrified replica of Rebecca, as one of the men nearest to the assault attempted to intercede. Unfortunately, he was only able to advance a step before one look from Durius turned him into dust. Fearing they would be next, the rest fled in terror.

When satisfied that the light had completely disappeared from the woman's eyes, Durius released her grip from her shattered neck, which allowed the corpse to drop to the ground. Not satisfied, a sword materialized in her hand, which she then used to pin her next victim against the wall. "With you it will not be so quick." With each slice of the blade, Durius drank in the image of Rebecca screaming as her sliced-open arteries emptied her blood onto the pavement.

Durius continued with every known weapon in the human arsenal employed to achieve each new death until at last the onslaught satiated the blood-soaked berserker.

———◆———

"I'd complain, for all the good that will do." Alicia looked over her new surroundings. "Channeling Maren O'Hara again are we?"

"Who can argue with the classics, though I had nothing consciously to do with it." Sean took Alicia by the hand and walked her through the front door. "Everything but Sean Thornton and Michaleen Oge Flynn."

Alicia started to crack up. "Sean and Thornton?"

Sean pulled her down onto the couch, and then tenderly kissed her lips.

Alicia reached her hands behind his back and arched hers to fit his body. "It's been a long time since we were alone, tiger." She moved her hand to unzip his pants, but his hand intercepted her attempt.

"I may be paranoid, but once you have your mind opened up like a can of tuna for all to see, the idea of being alone becomes a joke. How long have I been gone anyway?" After one hundred years of relative stability in the 1492 reality, Sean remembered time moved differently between realities.

"Sweetheart, I don't have any concept of time to compare it to considering the places I've been while you were gone. For all I know it could have been ten minutes or ten days." Alicia sat up and straightened her clothes. "It is a sad state of affairs if all a superior race has to do with their time is to watch us copulate."

For the next hour, they shared what each had gone through after Sean had disappeared into the stream of colors. "So what do you think they are trying to do?"

Sean shrugged his shoulders. "My best guess is that Carl is trying to impress his peers with his creation. Yet on the other side, my thought processes are changing. I perceive and remember things with a clarity that I used to dream of having. If I don't screw it up by thinking too hard about it, whatever I want is always right there."

"At least there seems to be a purpose in what Carl is doing with you, while I feel like someone who is sent in whenever a feminine touch is needed. I wonder if it is because my turn simply hasn't come up yet?"

As if in tune with the universe, they heard a familiar voice. Carl had materialized in the cottage doorway, once again in his Service Dress Whites. "It's interesting Alicia that you asked that particular question at this time, because you are up."

However, Sean didn't care for the sound of that. "Up for what? And why is it every time you come for one of us, you're in your Dress Whites?"

"It does not concern you, and I wear these clothes to remind you that we served together for a number of years."

Sean shot off the couch. "Like hell it doesn't concern me."

Alicia instantly reacted. "I know you didn't mean that the way it came out."

Flabbergasted, Sean yelled, "What?"

Though Alicia knew that before the crazy times, Sean had never played the White Knight role. However, lately his inner Tony had come out more often, and she was sick of it. "Since when do you feel the need to answer for me? And since when do you feel it is your place to decide for me what I can decide to do or decide not to?"

"Wow," Sean thought, "who knew that a simple emotional response to an idea that would endanger my wife could become a bigger headache than aliens peering into my darkest secrets?"

Then Sean sheepishly replied, "A mere slip of the male ego, honey. Sorry won't happen again."

Carl sat down next to Alicia, as a plate full of steaming shelled lobster tails appeared on the table. "Glad we got that settled."

Carl picked up one of the tails, and took a bite. "Actually there isn't any other choice, because analyzing the consciousness of humanity without the female viewpoint would be similar to eating this lobster without melted butter."

"So where's the butter?" Alicia realized she was starving, but before she could grab a lobster tail, a bowl of drawn butter appeared next to the lobster. "Thanks. So when is this supposed to happen?"

And what am I supposed to do while she goes star tripping?" Sean impatiently whined.

"Enjoy the lobster." Carl was about to leave them alone, when he felt the same disturbance that Sean Anthony had perceived in the containment room. "Sorry to cut this short, Admirals, but you've got to go."

Before either Sean or Alicia could say a word of goodbye to each other, they disappeared, leaving Carl alone in the hut. "It looks as if she took the bait." Carl took the last of the lobster and dipped it in the butter before he bit into it. "Now let's see how far she runs with it."

———◆———

"It's time for us to go." The sense of urgency in Sean Anthony's voice betrayed his concern for his family's immediate safety.

Rebecca read this to mean something new was coming. "What now?"

Before her son could answer, Adonis ran in from the server room. "Sean Anthony, I just received news that there is an unidentified aircraft, five hundred miles out and headed our way. Are they friendlies?"

"I'm afraid not." Sean Anthony turned to his mother. "Remember the Nazi task force you destroyed?"

"What, they're back?"

"Same idea, though this time much worse."

A worried Adonis asked, "Are we all going to turn into goop? I mean, if that's the case, I for one would prefer a rapid change in location."

He then ran back into the server room and came back with a stack of laptops. "Wherever we're going, these come with me." He clutched them tight to his chest and waited.

Rebecca wasn't ready to leave. "I told you last time, this is our home."

"No offense Mom, but home has become ground zero, and because we made it so, there isn't an adequate military deterrence to head off what will be overhead in the next thirty minutes. We have to go – now."

Rebecca was adamant. "Not yet, we don't."

Phoenix looked at Rebecca and realized what her mother had in mind and asked Sean Anthony. "The containment field. You did say when we built it that it had the capacity to cover a much wider area than what we needed to hide what we were doing. Could it be reconfigured to cover the city?"

This wasn't what Carl had in mind when he warned Sean Anthony of the different threats that could come their way and what the proper responses should be. "Protecting only New York doesn't change that we have nothing to counter the threat."

"It does if we can reverse the field and use it as an electromagnetic disrupter. All we have to do is reverse the polarity." Rebecca looked to Phoenix for confirmation.

Without waiting to explain, Phoenix shouted to Adonis, "Power up the containment field and crank up the amps from the grid."

Then to Sean Anthony she asked, "Would it be possible to utilize the energy from the current you pulled their friends out of?"

"To what end?" Sean Anthony for all of his immeasurable abilities could not grasp where Phoenix headed.

Rebecca explained. "We may have to go, but why not preserve the deconstructed mass rather than let them irradiate it before we leave. I am assuming of course that the threat is a nuclear bomb. By the way, is it me, or are we running out of places we can run to?"

"Break it to save it." Sean Anthony considered if there were any downsides to the idea. He decided, either way deconstructed or destroyed made little difference in the overall scheme of things, except to those carrying out the attack. "You have exactly ten minutes before we leave, finished or not."

Phoenix grabbed Rebecca's arm and pulled her into the server room where Adonis furiously typed commands. "I'll write the code to reverse the polarity while Adonis brings the containment field online. How much time?"

Adonis checked the power levels on one of the overhead monitors. "Containment in three minutes."

Phoenix pointed to Rebecca. "You go over there and bypass the heat sensors and surge protectors on everything in this room. The amount of power we need to expand the field will eventually melt down every piece of electronic equipment in this room."

All three of the techno geeks raced to perform their tasks with Adonis the first to claim success two and a half minutes later.

He yelled out to Sean Anthony in the containment room, "Containment achieved," which once again miraculously expanded in size to accommodate the surging mass. "Well I guess here is where we find out if your Dad agrees."

Moments later, a steady stream of the foreign matter began to stream from one of the walls. Two minutes later the flow reached its previous volume.

"You've got five minutes," Sean Anthony cautioned.

Rebecca then jubilantly announced. "Both heat and power

sensors are bypassed." Adonis and Rebecca turned their chairs to face Phoenix. "Whenever you're ready."

"I have to reroute power past the capacitors, and then we can get the hell out of Dodge." Phoenix then had a horrible thought. "What about Lydia?"

Sean Anthony was ahead of her. "Don't worry; I'll grab her on the way out."

Sean Anthony didn't give them time to think about the lives of the people they were about to irrevocably change, as everybody but him disappeared. He watched as the multi-colored stream rapidly expand throughout the basement before he too disappeared to pick up his daughter.

Exactly five minutes later, the center of New York City and everything in it deconstructed under the expanding stream. By the time the attacking bomber came within range of the city and released its nuclear payload, no landmarks remained to identify the sprawling metropolis. Instead of the normal blast and the accompanying mushroom cloud one would expect, as soon as the blast reached the ground, the deconstructed mass exploded skyward and permeated the entire blast radius.

In the blink of an eye, and to the astonishment of those who had released the weapon, the most beautiful rainbow of all of the colors in the spectrum thirty miles wide, and thirty thousand feet high, painted the sky. If you blinked, you missed it as the entire mass collapsed back to the ground.

Unfortunately for those Durius chose to carry out the attack, the connection to the deconstructed 2018 reality continued to pour into this 1942 reality, and rapidly spread its way throughout the Western Hemisphere undoing all of the work Rebecca and the rest of those from the Enterprise Task Force who remained behind spent the last 77 years building.

For those flying above not only was there nothing left to destroy, but to their horror, since the deconstructed mass had consumed everything, including the carrier they had launched from, they had nowhere to land.

Three hours later, after the aircraft ran out of fuel and dropped into the deconstructed soup, the entire 1942 reality and the 2018 reality became one massive Petri dish.

None of it came close to satisfying Durius; for once again, the main target of her wrath had escaped. She reached out with her senses to pick up any trace of where Rebecca and her friends had gone. From the obvious places, like an interdimensional jump into another reality, to distant places in time connected to the one she had just destroyed, her rage grew as the search proved fruitless. As Durius fumed, she noticed that company had arrived. "You can't keep her hidden from me forever."

Darius couldn't agree more. "True, but only long enough to end this charade. Because you think you can disrupt any dimension I may send them doesn't mean I'm out of options." Darius stood calmly next to his former mate. "You certainly have gone to great lengths for such little gain."

Durius didn't bother to face him. "Oh, it's really nothing. I could have sent a swarm of asteroids and left nothing for you to put back together, so why don't you save both of us the trouble and let me end her. If you do, I might allow the rest to live."

Darius countered. "After the many years you spent bringing violence and destruction to Earth, if you had a little more patience, you would have discovered that I was ready to crash the system anyway. Instead, you now need to sway those in the Continuum who have taken a closer look at what humanity could offer without your interference."

Durius finally turned her angry gaze his way. "What makes you think they care what happens to your silly little creatures?"

"I don't know, why don't we ask them and find out?" Darius

maintained a straight face as Durius fell into the rhetorical trap.

Durius laughed. "Do you think after they find out what your creatures are made of they would agree to give them greater abilities to spread their filth throughout the quadrant?"

"Couldn't hurt to try," Darius replied. "You of all creatures know what they could be capable of if you hadn't spent so much of your time helping them destroy themselves. The beauty of their art, music, literature, and most importantly, their drive has survived all of your best efforts to stamp them out."

The sky in front of the two became alive with marble sculptures and paintings from the Renaissance masters. Right behind came a troop of ballet dancers moving to the sounds of Swan Lake, and to their left Ella Fitzgerald in her prime belting out *Dream a Little Dream*.

All around them artists, architectural wonders, graceful Clipper sailing ships in full sail, geniuses from Einstein, Madame Currie, Tesla, and Archimedes popped in and out, and finally the adventurers who continually pushed the boundaries of the known world and beyond into space.

Darius continued. "What is truly sad about what could have been is you were the one responsible for most of those who possessed the gifts that aggressively pushed the boundaries of human understanding."

"And then you had to go screw it all up." Durius violently waved her outstretched hands and all of the images shattered and disappeared. "But then again, you have the same faults as your human pets in that they also breed pets that will be subservient and stand in for the lack of fulfilling relationships among their own kind."

Durius thought for a moment before she added, "I take that back. Unlike you, they at least let their pets die, and then they go find a new one."

"I suppose the irony is lost on you that by the acts of jealousy and revenge you spend most of your days mired in, you have become much like those you wish to destroy than the partner who was capable of such beauty."

Then Darius had to add. "As if this wasn't bad enough, for the first time in thousands of years you turned one of our kind into a one-dimensional killing machine whose mission in life is to despise everything he comes into contact with."

Durius wasn't impressed. "So now you are concerned for the offspring you chose to forfeit in favor of your half-breed one? How touching and revisionist of you."

Darius shook his head negatively. "You can't see that we even argue like humans. So rather than continue with this farce, I will remind you that through it all, not once have I interfered with any of your constructs on planets only you control."

Durius laughed at Darius' veiled threat. "The Continuum would never give you approval to do so and you know that."

It was Darius' turn to laugh. "Except you decided to enter my realms and wreak havoc on them, or did you conveniently believe that you are the only one capable of tracking interdimensional interactions?"

The smile faded from Durius' face. "You are forgetting that I have as much right to decide the fate of humanity as you do. They are every bit my creation as yours."

"Cromulus, Kalius, Surius, and Perculus also share equally in how humanity came into being. Why don't we let them have a say?"

As Darius stated their names, the four imprinters appeared next to them.

"We thought you'd never ask."

"This is not the time for you to have an opinion, Perculus."

Then to the others, Durius warned. "You've shown no interest in our affairs with the humans since that horrible day when as a favor to Darius you imprinted your individual talents. If you want to become involved now, I can only assume you wish to make an enemy of me."

Cromulus took exception. "I'd like to think I have been a little more active than you claim."

"So what?" Durius scoffed. "We've seen how much influence your messages of love and compassion mattered. Every time I ran out of new ways to expose these silly creatures, the easiest manipulation at my disposal was to throw up an image of you as Jesus, and then publish something nasty about whom I wished to have suffer. Blacks marrying whites? An easy mashup of Bible verses – done. New laws prohibiting gay marriage? Check. Hell, I successfully used Jesus to glorify every act of evil humanity has perpetrated. If not for the humor of witnessing such naked hypocrisy, without Jesus, no one would have spent a second thinking about traveling here to be entertained."

"Also the reason so many became bored with the repetitious religious oppression, destruction, and slaughter. Your constant meddling made it impossible to enjoy the other elements we brought to their nature." Kalius appeared as one of the Goddesses from Olympus. In a sheer white robe that exposed every curve in her perfectly balanced body. She had definitely dressed for the occasion. The smile she directed toward Durius was to remind her of the envy Kalius knew had existed since they were children.

Her sister's assessment enraged Durius. "As pathetic as Cromulus' attempts to civilize these barbarians is, you're even worse. Wisdom? That is what you gifted? Let's see how many ways I can belittle your contribution. Oh, that's right, I never had to consider ways to neutralize such a nonexistent quality. At least before our involvement, as primates they had enough wisdom to work together to ensure their survival as a troop. Afterward, you take the same group and put them together on an island alone for a year and at least half would have slaughtered the other half."

Darius put up his hands in surrender. "Before you slander the contributions of Surius and Perculus, whether you like it or not, they are all involved in the outcome of the drama you set in motion.

By the way, once I told them what I had in mind they didn't need any convincing."

Surius spoke for the first time. "I'm looking forward to it." Contrary to the others present, his appearance was small and meek. No one would have mistaken him for anything other than one of the hundreds of extras that filled in the scenery around the main characters in a movie, completely forgettable.

Perculus agreed. "I had some free time, and it sounds like fun." She had chosen to look and dress in a manner that accentuated a confidence in her intellect that others would want to emulate. In other words, she was similar in nature to Durius, except without all of her current baggage.

"Enough!" Durius poked her index finger angrily into Darius' chest. "What *exactly* do you have in mind?"

Cromulus answered for Darius. "It's rather an ingenious idea if you ask me. Instead of you two continuing to beat the shit out of each other, and making who knows how many worlds uninhabitable for the next million years in the process, why not let those who helped create the humans decide if there is potential?"

Darius looked around to see heads nodding in the affirmative. "They all agree. What about it? Are you willing to take a chance on the wisdom of our peers?"

Unimpressed, Durius answered. "Why should I agree? Maybe I don't have a problem with blowing as many worlds into oblivion as I want to."

Darius' tone hardened. "Because if you don't agree, I will return in kind to those worlds you do value, and we both know which ones I will target first."

Any civilization, no matter how advanced, has inner secrets known only to those responsible for its creation. As a couple, Darius and Durius had spent millions of years sharing these secrets with each other. The irony was that the worlds Durius had populated with creatures were paradises compared to those others had

127

Where Are We Now?

created. Outside of her hatred of all things human, Durius was the model of perspective and balance in nature.

Durius pouted. "I hate you."

Darius smiled. "I can live with that."

Durius took a moment to collect her thoughts before returning to his proposal. "None of this matters if the members of the Continuum judge the examples of humanity you send them lacking. Regardless of what judgments occur among us, their decision still ends this."

Darius knew there was a *but* coming. "And if they accept them as worthy?"

"Then all of the rest of you here have to reach the same conclusion. If any *one* of you agrees with me that the human experiment is a gross failure and should disappear from time, that will also be sufficient to end their miserable existence."

Once again, Darius read her reaction correctly. "I can live with that as well, except for one little addendum."

Durius wanted to wipe the smile he still had right off his face. "And?"

"You will be the one to judge the one whom you have sown."

She didn't see that coming. "What, so I can take it apart piece by piece and throw it in your face?"

"No, so maybe you could learn a little understanding from someone who shares your strengths and weaknesses. Who knows, you might even learn something about yourself."

Darius then turned his attention to all of the imprinters. "No harm comes to those we test. All in, or we continue as is."

Even with the knowledge that Rebecca wouldn't be the one who stood before her, under her breath Durius reluctantly agreed. "Remember all it takes is for one of you to agree with me." She specifically directed these words at her sister Kalius.

Kalius put her hand on her sister's shoulder. "Regardless of whether it goes your way or not, my hope is that once this is over, you will focus your attention in a more constructive manner. It's been an infinitely long time since I've been able to enjoy my real sister, and I would love to have her back."

For the first time in ages, Durius' stern countenance softened. Without speaking, she communicated directly with Kalius. "I would love nothing better than to be cruising through a Super Nova again with you, but I will make you pay if you don't help me with this."

With a look of *yeah right*, Kalius reminded her sister, "Like the last time you were in my position mattered to you? As I recall, you did nothing to keep my darling Emdians from extinction."

"Touché."

Satisfied and surprised at how swiftly they all had reached agreement, Darius left.

Cromulus shook his head as he stated sarcastically, "You have to admit, the man knows how to make an exit."

The End of Part I

Part II
Are We Not Worthy?

Kalius stood alone in Renée's Colorado ranch house living room. She realized her sexually intimidating appearance wouldn't do, so she changed to more conservative attire.

At that moment, Renée walked through the front door and froze when she saw the striking woman standing in front of her. "Now who the hell are you?"

Kalius didn't bother to respond, as she smiled and entered Renée's consciousness. "Relax Renée. We're going to take a trip down memory lane."

Renée felt her identity rapidly peeling away layer by layer until the only memory left was when Kalius imprinted her thousands of years earlier. Millions of memories then flowed through from then until the present.

"No wonder everything is so messed up." For the first time since a child, Renée could see beyond the clutter of day-to-day life to remember the vision of her place in the universe. "Whoever said wisdom is a by-product of age definitely had their head up their ass."

Kalius disavowed her of that notion. "What you observed is a small fraction of all you have experienced throughout 27,000 years of life experiences. Don't be fooled. That you are now aware of an early realization of the miracle of life does not mean you were able to understand it then. You are experiencing your emotional memories, aided by what we share."

None of this made any sense to Renée. "To what end?"

"Honestly, on whether or not I remove my imprint from your DNA."

With all of her primitive humanity stripped away, Renée remained remarkably at ease with the idea, except for one thing. "Can I keep him if you decide everything else is a waste of time?"

"Unfortunately, that is out of my hands. Your Tony has his own ordeal to face. Shall we continue?"

<hr />

Another reality away, Alicia sat at her desk in the Pentagon when she was Secretary of Defense. On the other side sat a diminutive man, who definitely looked out of place. "Okay, I now know whoever is running the show has lost their marbles. So who are you, and what's up with the silly grin?"

"What? No question about why here?"

"Yeah, like when have I ever received an honest answer to that question?" Alicia asked sarcastically.

"I can see you want everything up front, so here we go. My name is Surius, and I am responsible for imprinting myself on your particular lineage. Now I am here to determine if you get to keep it."

"And why here?" Alicia felt a headache coming on.

Surius put his feet up on the desk. "No reason other than this was at the apex of your professional life, and the décor suits me."

"Okay, so what's next? You shred me into a billion pieces and inspect all the parts? Or is this another magical mystery tour?"

"You ready?" Surius got out of his seat and made his way to the door.

"Do I have a…"

Alicia lay on her childhood bed, mesmerized by the small ponytailed child staring back at her. Even with all of her adult memories intact, she had no control over her childhood emotions. "Daddy!"

Then came the sound of footsteps running up the stairs and the door violently swing open. "What's wrong Princess?"

Though the once imposing figure of Alicia's father now lacked the aura of invincibility, in the 4-year-old's mind, the man she hadn't seen for over twenty years brought a stream of tears down her cheeks. Without a thought, she rushed over and threw her arms around him with a grip he had never known. "What is it? Did you have a nightmare?"

"I don't know." Alicia became suspicious, and released her grip. She spent an uncomfortable amount of time staring at her father's face, before she pushed him away. "This isn't real. I am a fully grown woman, and you've been gone for some time." This may be what she thought, but what came out were the rambling sounds of an overly excited 4-year-old.

The look of sympathy from this man masquerading as her father became immaterial when her memory of how devastating it was to lose the family's dog, slammed into her. "It's all right, Allie. We all miss Chester," her father consoled.

This first soul crushing memory of her life brought another round of tearful sobbing, with her hands covering her face.

Another shock awaited Alicia when she looked up again to see her adult self in the mirror, and Surius instead of her father in the reflection. "That was extremely cruel."

"I'm sorry if you believed it would be otherwise." The man looked so fragile that a gust of wind could blow him away. Short stringy hair box cut around the ears matched perfectly with a face so pockmarked only a mother could love it. When he smiled at Alicia, crooked yellow-stained teeth stared back at her. "Personally speaking, the only Alicia I want to get to know is the one who manages to take on the emotions of others and still have the capacity to make practical decisions. So expect more of the same."

Before she could object, she became a passenger in the cab of an old pickup truck. Alicia recognized the interior of the restored

1971 Chevy that belonged to her first serious boyfriend, and the 17-year-old behind the wheel did not look happy. As usual when Matt lost it, the music was so loud it made conversation nearly impossible, which added to the tension.

"Holy shit. One of the worst days of my life. Thanks a lot."

"You're welcome. But I think you know there is more to come on this particularly bad day."

"Great. So you are going to stay in my head? By the way, who did you say your name was?"

"The name is Surius, and you already know who I am. Anyway, I know that you have not forgotten how miserable you were for the six months you spent trying to break up with this jerk. Why do you think you had so much trouble dumping this sexist moron?"

Before she could suppress it, the whole six months scrolled through Alicia's consciousness. "His mother treats him like shit; no dad; he's my first and I thought I loved him; it will break his heart; he might hurt me."

Alicia could see Matt yelling above the music, but she could not hear the words. Her body tensed up to prepare for a physical assault. At that moment, she realized the time had come to take a stand. She reached over and turned off the stereo. "Listen asshole. I have had enough of your pity party. Stop this fucking truck right now and let me out!"

This further enraged the young man, who reacted by reaching over to grab Alicia's hair. Instead, all he got was a hand of empty air. In a case of instant karma, with Alicia no longer there to stop his forward movement, he lost control of the steering wheel and at fifty miles an hour the pristine 1971 Chevy left the road and took out several saplings before hitting one mature enough to stop the truck cold. Fortunately for the dazed Matt, he would recover from the experience; however, his beloved truck did not.

When she disappeared, Alicia returned to the bedroom with the pathetic looking Surius. "You stayed because you lacked the tools to separate your needs from those of the one who was your first love. Now, how about this one?"

The 16-year-old Alicia flipped him her middle finger. "I hate you."

To which Surius gleefully replied, "I know, isn't this great."

⁓

Franklin looked up from his newspaper. "I think company is on the way."

Tony jumped off the couch. "It's about time. Another day alone with you and I would agree to eat a bowl of peas if it would free me from staring at your ugly mug."

No sooner had Tony finished insulting Franklin, than Rebecca, Phoenix, her daughter Lydia, and Adonis arrived in the usual flash of green mist. Disappointed with who was not with them, Tony demanded, "For the love of God, Franklin, where is René? And who are all of these people?"

Franklin stood up and walked over to the new arrivals. "Well first off Tony, you know Rebecca, so let me introduce you to Phoenix, Sean Anthony's wife, their daughter Lydia, and Adonis who I have no idea why he is still party to this story."

Tony ignored the introductions. "So where is Renée?"

Franklin ignored Tony and addressed Rebecca. "I do believe your presence is required elsewhere."

Before she could protest, Rebecca disappeared in a green flash.

"Now, to answer your question Tony, Renée is in the middle of some important negotiations that will hopefully shed some light on how all of this turns out for everybody."

Tony shook his head in disgust. "Listen asshole, even for you that has to be the worst mouthful of horseshit I've ever heard."

"I can only give you what I get, Tony. As far as anyone in this room is concerned, consider yourselves on standby until you are not." A bottle of the finest 18th Century French Burgundy appeared in Franklin's hand and glasses for everybody else in theirs. "What say we make the most out of it?"

"And these three?" Tony's tone was dismissive of the strangers.

With that, Adonis got in his face. "Two of us happen to be responsible for there still being anyone left alive is who *these* people are. A better question would be who are you, and where are we?"

Phoenix stepped in front of her friend. "It's okay big guy, I have looked the place over, and as you can see there are pictures of him with Renée, Sean, and Alicia on the mantle above the fireplace. We're in the 1492 reality version of Cuba, and this must be Captain Anthony Knox."

Fortunately for all concerned, Franklin had removed the severed heads.

Phoenix put her hand out to Tony. "Glad to meet you."

Skeptically Tony took it. "How do you know any of that?"

"Long story, but the short version is Rebecca Eddington is my mother-in-law, and Adonis here happens to be one of the most badass hackers in any dimension."

Tony loosened up a bit. "Yes, I remember Franklin told us earlier about you helping to pull us out of the soup. Thanks for that."

"You are welcome." Phoenix then turned to Franklin and spent a moment looking him up and down. "Good to see you again, Dr. Franklin, and thank you for pulling us out of 2018 when it was all going to hell."

"My pleasure."

With Renée still gone and Franklin's half-assed explanation about where she was, Tony grabbed the bespectacled Franklin by his arm and steered him toward the kitchen. "You three stay here."

Once there, he demanded, "Start making sense, or so help me."

Franklin lowered his head so his eyes peered above his glasses and his mischievous smile returned. "Well since you are now all grown up, it wouldn't hurt to let you know your turn is coming soon."

"My turn? My turn for what?"

"I can't say, so why don't we return to our guests so you can get to know them." Though Franklin knew Tony's time was short, he didn't know exactly how short.

Tony knew he wouldn't get anything more out of Franklin, so he stated the obvious. "As long as you can assure me that Renée is all right."

Franklin gave Tony a look of disgust before finally lowering the hammer. "You should have figured out by now that anyone of us could die at any time, and you are asking me is she *all right*? Hell no, she is not *all right*. None of us are *all right*, so please do all of us a big favor and stop asking that stupid question."

As Tony stood stunned over the rebuke, Franklin added, "For the moment though, she is having the time of her life."

Tony looked Franklin over before he decided how to reply. As much as he wanted to fire back, he could clearly see that he had become a whiny baby when it came to Renée. "You are right, and I'll work on it. So where is it I am supposed to be going?"

Franklin's expression conveyed the usual.

"I know, you can't tell me."

<hr />

When he awoke from a deep sleep, most confused of all was Captain Daniel Osaka. One minute he was with his family sailing on the Chesapeake Bay happily retired after seventy-five years of service, and the next minute on the bridge of his former command, the Enterprise. When the Enterprise Task Force began to sink into the alien currents of color, he arrived in a pasture with Tony, Renée, and Franklin only to have the green mist envelope him once again.

As he observed his strange new environment, he yelled in frustration, "What the hell is this?"

"Some would say Shangri-La; though that is a myth I created some time long ago."

Osaka turned around to see a young woman dressed in a simple printed peasant wrap. A slight breeze rose throwing up millions of flower petals scattered throughout the landscape. Instead of asking for an explanation from the girl, Osaka remained in silent awe as the swirling flower petals began to take the shape of a dragon. In fascination, he watched as a majestic set of wings unfurled from both sides of its body before the dragon flew up high in the sky.

When it was almost a speck in the early morning sky, it pirouetted on one wing to begin a steep dive. When the dragon reached the ground, it opened its mouth wide to devour the girl, and then explode back into millions of individual petals.

Osaka had a difficult time separating the conflicting emotions the scene evoked. "Shangri-La all right, with a little Hitchcock mixed in."

With no one around and nothing but beautiful vistas everywhere he looked, Osaka wandered around the strange new environment as he pondered the meaning of the little girl and the flower petal dragon. He then picked a suitable location to sit down and wait for what might come next. Oddly, he wondered, "Should I give some thought to what has come of those under my command?"

Satisfied with the spot, he laid back against a well-worn boulder. After a few minutes in the cool mountain air and with nothing to react to, his eyes closed and Daniel Osaka fell back into a deep sleep.

Cromulus spent a few moments observing the peaceful scene before he decided he had seen enough. "I don't need to explore this gentle soul any further, at least for now."

———◆———

After he and Alicia disappeared from the Irish cottage, Sean sat at a sidewalk café a block away from the Eiffel Tower in Paris. Though the Sun in the sky signified that it was midday, there wasn't another soul in sight.

Sean smiled as he thought, "Since the first time I watched Cary Grant and Grace Kelly in *To Catch a Thief*, I've had a special affinity for this place."

"Mine was when Humphrey Bogart said goodbye to Ingrid Bergman in Casablanca, just before Paris fell to the Nazis."

Sean turned his view from the Eiffel Tower to where a voice came from. "Nazis again? Seems to be a reoccurring theme."

"What can I say? If I were born in Gaul during Caesar's rampage, it would be the Romans. Simply a victim of my environment I guess."

Sean picked up the glass of wine in front of him, and took a sip. "So, I'm not familiar with your particular voice in my head. Care to introduce yourself?"

"Ironic that all of the forms of diversion you chose to occupy your mind with, escapism and humor dominate. Yet in your music tastes, you run headlong into the most rebellious influences, which you then contradict with some of the most beautiful contemporary pieces of pop. You my friend are all over the map."

Sean chuckled. "Just one big mass of contradictions."

"Would you change an unfavorable outcome if you possessed the power to do so?"

Behind the question, Sean instinctively knew he better be careful of his answer. "Let's see. From everything I've learned over the last 155 years living through three different realities and surviving, is that my place in the universe hasn't given me much of a choice in the outcome, and this case would be no different."

"Not what I expected."

"Life never is."

"Would you wish to live forever?"

Sean laughed at where this one-sided conversation was headed. "Having never done so, how would I know? How do you like living forever?"

"Cheeky. Your kind seems to be obsessed with the idea."

Between the thousands of unknown voices in his head while he traveled through his memories and the constant manipulations of those he cared about, Sean was at the end of his patience. "Yes, and your kind make the idea of a shortened existence welcoming.

I know I would rather not be in a position where life became an exercise in tearing off butterfly wings simply because I could. Walk a mile in my shoes, and all."

"I can't say that I blame you. Then what say we get to the business at hand."

As the unidentified voice finished, the surrounding Parisian landscape disappeared, and Sean now hovered one hundred yards above the swirling currents of color he had witnessed earlier.

"Are you ready to feel what it's like to become a creator?"

This was the last thing Sean wanted. "Sure, just like I want to be a restaurant owner in Gordon Ramsay's sights," Sean said sarcastically.

Instead of a reply, structures began to form out of the deconstructed mass. Within seconds a lone restaurant stood, with the front door opening and a familiar figure emerging. "That was the worst excuse for a Rack of Lamb I ever tasted. If you don't get your shi…"

To Sean's surprise, with the thought of making the horrific sight go away, both the restaurant and the maniacal chef dropped back into the currents.

"Peaceful thoughts, only peaceful, relaxing thoughts." As Sean repeated this mantra, a stunning mountain range complete with a large crystal blue lake rose up around him. "That's more like it."

He sat down to contemplate his next move, which came in seconds. "Alicia."

Nothing. "Tony, Renée, anyone?" Still nothing.

The sound of trees rustling in his periphery caught Sean's attention. He was about to go over to check it out, when a ten point stag cautiously poked his head out from behind one of the trees. The second he processed this idea, in rapid succession a black bear with two cubs in tow showed up to the north, a flock of geese flew overhead, and a couple of frisky grey squirrels wound their way up the pine tree directly behind him.

"So I can imagine into reality my environment, but I can't do the same for people? Well, let's try…"

Before he could finish speaking the words, a white shack with a neon sign above it bearing a heart with the word Cupid materialized in front of him. A pimple-faced young man wearing a black bow tie and white paper hat peered out of the counter window. Oddly, the young man didn't seem confused at all by his strange surroundings. "What'll you have?"

"Note to self, make that people I know." Sean leaned over the counter to see the familiar six-slotted board used to cradle the completed hot dogs as ordered. "What the hell, why not. Three with mustard, onions, and chili to go."

"That will be five and a half dollars."

Sean reached into his pocket, pulled out a five and two ones and handed them over. "Keep the change."

No sooner had he picked his dogs off the counter than the shack disappeared and a recliner chair materialized next to him. "So I'll eat my hot dogs, enjoy the scenery, and hopefully an idea will arrive about how I'm supposed to deal with all of this."

Renée woke up feeling strange. She could not remember going to sleep, and when she went to check the time on her alarm clock, it wasn't there. She sat up in bed to examine the room. "This is not my room. Where am I this time? Oh well, at least my thoughts are mine again."

She continued to survey her new surroundings and realized this was a room of privilege. High exposed beam ceiling with intricate scrollwork back dropped colorful tapestries and fine handcrafted furniture. This, along with the silk nightgown she wore informed her that wherever she was, she didn't lack for much. "What a beautiful place, but where is the bathroom?"

A polite knock on the door coincided with the discovery of

a chamber pot that sat on a marble top dresser. "Why do I keep winding up in places without indoor plumbing and toilet paper? You have got to be kidding me."

The knock on the door became more insistent as Renée struggled to accept the rudimentary hygiene. "Give me a minute."

A nervous male voice responded. "As you ordered, the council of ministers is waiting in the throne room for Your Highness. Daphne is also waiting here to dress you."

"What the hell? Your Highness?" Renée frantically ran to the large window that took up most of the far wall and threw open the twelve foot high curtains. To her amazement, she discovered the most beautifully manicured estate she could imagine. Horse-drawn carriages stretched nearly a half a mile along the cobblestone road, and a large contingent of soldiers stood in formation on the expansive lawn. "Your Highness of what? What kind of fairy tale am I in now?"

Renée took a deep breath and in her most authoritarian voice commanded, "Send her in."

One of the massive double doors swung open, and a rather rotund middle-aged woman aggressively marched into the room with an armful of garments. "As much as it is your right to proceed at your own pace, you must know today is much too important to diddle Your Majesty." She walked over and placed the clothing on the bed before she motioned for Renée to come to her.

Left without another obvious choice, Renée did as ordered.

Over the next hour, the ordeal exposed every one of Renée's private parts to the ten handmaidens it apparently took to prepare her for the audience that waited. Throughout, Renée tried to discern the identity of her character, but received only a curtsy from the intimidated servants as they made their way in and out of the bedchamber.

When they finally completed the task, Renée's appearance emanated royal power. From the bright red, hooped silk dress and the fortune of gold and gems around her neck and arms to the crown on her head, the final appearance put to shame most other Royals throughout the ages. However, the laced up whalebone corset one particularly brutish servant pulled tight around her torso made it impossible to draw a complete breath of air.

Daphne nodded her head in approval and dismissed the rest of the staff. "Sir Francis awaits."

With more confidence than she had a right to feel, Renée shook her head in agreement.

Daphne snapped her fingers and in strode Sir Alfred Frances, in full military peacock attire. "The Ambassador of Remaria is growing impatient, Your Majesty. We must hurry."

"Remaria? So I was right, this isn't real. Big help. Okay, fake it until you make it time," Renée thought. One of the many things Renée had learned over four hundred years of holding a world together is never let the facts get in the way of what you are doing.

After Renée scrutinized the man, one thing was obvious. "It certainly does not help that the ambassador witnessed you sweating like a pig, Sir Frances. I suppose the rest of my council is equally uncomfortable?"

"He is threatening to cross our borders if you don't give him your answer forthwith, Your Highness."

"Good. A point of reference," she thought. "Assemble my council in the dining hall at once. Send the ambassador my compliments, and that I will allow him an audience one hour from now."

Sir Frances stopped short. "But Your Highness…"

Renée gave him a look she assumed he would construe as *move it or die a horrible death*. The speed of his departure indicated it worked. "Now, it would be nice to know where the dining hall is."

Five minutes later and seated at the head of a twenty-six place table, Renée surveyed the male faces of entitlement and queried the group, "So who here can tell me why I should meet with the ambassador?"

"As you well know, Your Majesty, unless your daughter agrees to change her mind and marry Prince Caricature of Remaria, his father King Oblivious IV has promised to invade the Kingdom."

Renée could tell by the tone in his voice that the pompous man stating the threat resented giving his allegiance to her. Not only that, but Caricature and Oblivious? "How many of you at this table feel I should demand of my daughter to do so?"

Instead of directing his answer to the Queen, Lord Francis spoke directly to those seated. "None here believe the silly girl should be allowed to abrogate her responsibility to crown and country."

After unanimous nods of approval, he turned to Renée. "But you already knew this." Lord Francis then gleefully added, "Does this mean you have come to your senses, Your Majesty?"

Renée now understood two important pieces of the puzzle. One, the obnoxious Lord Francis wanted her throne and was probably responsible for the crisis, and two, she must have a really cool daughter. "Is King Oblivious with his army?"

"Are you well, Your Majesty?" This question came from the elderly Lord to her left, who seemed genially concerned. "We've known for the last week that he traveled at the head of his army, as he always has."

Renée had all she needed. "Thank you for your council." Without another word, the Queen exited the room, and to Daphne, who had waited outside of the room, she ordered, "Prepare my riding clothes and have the stable ready my horse." Seeing that Daphne couldn't decide what to do first, Renée made the decision for her. "See to the horse, I'll manage to dress myself."

Then Renée had another thought, which sent her in search of the throne room. Fortunately for her, it wasn't too difficult to find the most garish room in the palace. Totally confused by her frenetic energy, the Queen's ladies-in-waiting tried to keep up with her, along with some of the Lords who had never seen this side of her before.

As the Queen entered the large room, she paused to pick out the ambassador. Then without ceremony walked up to him and demanded, "You will accompany me back to your Lord's encampment. I'll be ready in twenty minutes." Renée then turned back to face her astonished Lords. "So Lord… Oh hell." Renée turned to the attendant closest to her and whispered, "What's his name?"

The nervous girl could barely speak. "Lord Hostilious, Your Majesty."

"Of course it is." On her way out of the stunned hall, Renée stopped next to him. "You are coming with me."

Before he could respond, she had turned her back to him and directed her attention to the elderly Lord who had earlier shown concern. "Make sure it is only the Queen's Guard that accompanies me, and if you believe it necessary, add your presence."

Lord Compassious was happy to comply with his more-in-command Queen than he had ever witnessed before. "I will be honored to ride with you, Your Majesty."

Exactly twenty minutes later and dressed to go on a Sunday ride in the country, Renée set out with her armed escorts. Along the way, she made a point to observe Lord Hostilious. His miserable countenance made her smile.

Two miles from the Queen's estate, they crested a hill that overlooked the valley below where a military encampment stretched its entire breath. "Well here goes nothing. Stay here." She then ordered the ambassador, "You, come with me." Without waiting his response or arguing against strong objections from Lord Compassious, Renée dug her heels into her horse and in full gallop raced away from her protectors.

As they rapidly closed the distance with the flags of both the Queen and the ambassador flapping in the wind, the sentries below remained frozen into inaction. This allowed the two clear passage straight through to the King's pavilion. Twenty yards from the tent, Renée brought her horse to a halt and in one fluid motion dismounted. "Queen…"

"Damn, I still don't know my name," she muttered under her breath. "Inform King Oblivious that the Queen is here for an audience with him."

She needn't have asked, as the flap on the tent folded open, and a short man with extremely large ears and nose to match emerged with his head at an unusual tilt. "What is the meaning of this? Have you come to restore my son's honor?"

Renée leaned in close. "Can we talk alone? I think I have an offer that will make both of our lives easier."

"Sire, this is an outrage. We gain nothing from this unless it is to acknowledge that Princess Aurora agrees to marry Prince Caricature. Anything else is a waste of your time."

King Oblivious wasn't in a hurry to begin a bloodbath. "Calm down Lord Kunninglious. Let us hear what she has to offer."

"There you are. Perfect," Renée thought, "Hostilious has a counterpart."

"He will never marry her if we decide to bash each other's brains out." Then under her breath to the King, Renée added, "Unless of course there are those who would win regardless of which one of us loses."

Fortunately for Renée's purpose, the King's body language indicated that he too wanted to avoid conflict. "I will hear what Queen Incredulous has to say."

He nodded and the tent flap pulled back, as the King motioned Renée to pass through it.

"Queen Incredulous, really?" In spite of the thought that this could be a dangerous situation, this absurd situation was more fun than Renée had experienced in quite some time.

Half an hour later, the two sovereigns exited the tent laughing. "No, I really didn't know you could do that. You are quite the scoundrel, my dearest King."

"If half of what you shared were true, my only wish would be to live long enough to try some of them myself." This brought another round of thoroughly unroyal laughter from the two.

Lord Hostilious had ridden into the encampment and stood waiting. When he saw how happy the Royals acted, he shot his counterpart an angry look before he asked in disbelief, "There will be no marriage?"

Renée's facial expression conveyed the obvious news. It also told him his days on the Queen's Council were numbered.

"Impossible." Lord Hostilious was quick to add. "You cannot let the Remarians challenge to Your Majesty's honor go without being avenged."

This brought the King's laughter to an abrupt end. "Contrary to your best attempts Lord Hostilious, there will be no war. However, there will be another battle in its stead." The King snapped his fingers and six members of his royal guard threw both Lord Hostilious and Lord Kunninglious to the ground and shackled their hands and legs.

"What is the meaning of this outrage?" Lord Kunninglious screamed, as he struggled against the weight of his attackers.

"Quite simple jackass. All the King and I had to do was have a little face to face to discover the horrible advice we each received from our military leaders." Renée paused to give Oblivious his turn.

"That and neither child wanted the marriage, and since all of the other Lords across both Kingdoms trade easy among each other, who is it that really cares?"

Now firmly in the grips of uncontrollable rage, Lord Hostilious spit out, "Between the two of us, we control the largest number of men in arms. You haven't a chance."

"That would have been true if both of your armies weren't busy facing each other. Thank you for that by the way. Besides your numbers pale in comparison to the other thirty odd Lords who want nothing to do with your war."

The King then addressed Renée. "Your dungeon or mine?"

Renée noticed the lighter moods of those who witnessed the most feared bullies of both realms were now in chains.

A grand celebratory feast occurred that evening that historians would talk about for centuries. However, Renée would not be around to attend it.

"That was quite impressive how you handled the unknown." Kalius' voice was back in her head. "FYI, the real Queen would have died a horrible death along with the Princess, and both Hostilious and Kunninglious would have taken both crowns only to devastate both Kingdoms trying to kill each other a few years later. Well done."

"Oblivious, Hostilious, and Queen Incredulous, really?" Renée responded.

"My world, my people."

Durius found Aaron in the first place she looked, sitting in a red crushed velvet booth surrounded by this world's version of strippers. "So you lose your head and come crawling into this hellhole."

Recognizing his mother, the females abruptly scattered. They had been on the wrong end of her particular brand of crazy before. Aaron didn't bother to look up. "Sure beats anything you've wasted my time with. So how goes the battle with Daddy Dearest?"

"Wrapping up shortly." Durius sat down next to Aaron and put her hand on his knee. "I know I've been rough on you, and I would like to make it up to you."

Aaron laughed. "What do you want? You have another world out there you need my particular talent to ruin?"

"No, only the one that you failed to finish off, and it might help you out to know your half-brother is the only one standing in your way. Well that is if you don't count the reptilian who cleaved your head from your neck and his twisted buddy." Durius' tone was equal parts challenging and soothing.

"What's in it for me?" Aaron looked up at his mother and rubbed two of his fingers together.

"Oh nothing, just your personal playground to inhabit with whatever turns you on."

"Not good enough. Besides, why would I care to follow in either of my parents footsteps, and I certainly don't need to be reminded how my half-blood brother managed to beat me." Aaron snapped his fingers at the waitress and pointed at his empty glass. "Besides, why don't you go do it yourself if it is so important to you."

"Because I have to be somewhere else, and we are running out of time."

For the first time in his life, Aaron noticed uncertainty in his mother's words. "We? In case you haven't noticed I could give a rat's ass." Then it hit him. "Dad's got you beat too."

Regardless of how frustrating it was to sit there and take Aaron's attempt at rebellion, Durius ignored the digs. "Regardless of whether or not you have any interest in my dispute your father, there is still a fantastic opportunity to hurt Sean Anthony. All you have to do is go to the only reality left habitable to them and bring a little something back for me."

Aaron downed the drink the waitress had placed in front of him, and ordered another. "Still don't hear what's in it for me. Oh wait, I know, a slap in the face and another round of emotional abuse when you are not satisfied that I met your lofty standards."

"His wife and her child are with him, and like me, Carl will be too busy elsewhere to come to the rescue."

This news piqued Aaron's interest. "When you say wife and child, I'm assuming like his father, Sean Anthony has gone native?" He laughed at what his mother had suggested. "For a race that has existed for billions of years, we should be more evolved than we are."

"And yet here we are. You'll do it?"

Aaron shook his head. "That depends on whether or not you give me what I want."

After Aaron finished spelling out what he wanted from Durius in return, she had to admit, she was surprised he had it in him. "I can promise to try, but you haven't exactly ingratiated yourself to those whose aid I'll need."

Aaron downed the fresh drink and threw the glass at the wall across the room; glass shards rained down over those seated underneath. "Not my problem. Shall we go?"

Rebecca slowly opened her eyes and gave a full body stretch, before she sat up and glanced around to find herself in the most wonderful lab she had ever seen. She busted up laughing at the juxtaposition of a king size bed in the middle of such a place and her pajamas covered in Minions. "Not quite my thing, but comical never the less."

"I didn't think you would appreciate hippie chic in nightwear."

"Thanks for that, I guess." Rebecca jumped off the bed and headed toward a bank of servers, or what she assumed were servers. There she observed a woman who looked to be in her mid-thirties literally perched on nothing with her feet up and resting on, well nothing.

"This is totally cool." Rebecca waved her hand under the strange woman's butt and then feet. "Did I say how totally cool this is. What is it? Controlled force fields, antigravity wells?"

Rebecca stared at the woman who, though smiling, remained silent. "Okay, I give. Who are you and where did you come by all this amazing equipment?"

"I engineered most of it." The stranger rose effortlessly and reached out her hand. "You can call me Perculus for the sake of better communication."

"You are the one who designed Specter," Rebecca stated as an absolute fact.

Perculus bowed low. "You don't know how hard it was to familiarize your husband with enough of the nuts and bolts of it to be able to use it. He's always been more the bioengineer type of creator."

"You know Carl?"

"You might say Darius and I go back a ways. However, this is the first time we worked together on a project. You might say I even had a hand in creating the circumstances that led to his finding you."

Her words got Rebecca to take a closer look at the woman. Average in shape and facial features, with brown hair pinned up in a bun, and if not for her eyes, she could be mistaken as a middle manager's personal secretary. "You have the most beautiful eyes I have ever seen. I feel if I looked into them long enough, I would see the entire universe."

Rebecca abruptly turned away while she rubbed her eyes vigorously. "Wow!

"Wait a minute. What did you mean when you said *led to finding me*?"

"Do the math sweetheart. You have shared enough personal insight with Darius to know he wasn't the only one responsible for humanity. Besides, if he did, wouldn't it be rather incestuous of him to be bonking you." Perculus made a motion with her hand and they were no longer in the lab.

Rebecca's remarkable mind understood most of the surreal scene that now played out all around her. Entranced and in awe she watched magnetic fields collide with radio waves as radiation from the Sun bombarded the area. Thousands of particles, some organic, others inorganic danced like fairies through the tapestry, as they swept in and out of currents of interstellar dust.

Added to this incredible image electricity in partnership with light particles raced alongside each other magnifying the scene in a brilliance Rebecca's senses could barely contain. Fantastic displays of every color of the rainbow lit up her mind in an orgy of ecstasy the likes of which were beyond human description.

"Is this how you perceive reality?" Rebecca's words came out in a whisper, as if spoken any louder the spell would be broken.

"If you mean can we see reality down to the smallest quark, then yes, this is one way we can look at reality."

Through Rebecca's mind, Perculus reached out her hand, which began to emit its own colorful array of colors. This produced an energy that opened up a clearing out to fifty feet that allowed their freedom of movement in the field.

Transfixed, Rebecca found for the first time in her life something so complex she could not think of a way to explain what she perceived.

Satisfied with Rebecca's reaction, Perculus let her enjoy the moment only long enough not to get lost in its majesty.

When the magic show abruptly ended, they returned to the lab. After a moment to allow her experience to permeate every corner of her consciousness, Rebecca exploded. "Why are you showing all of this to me? How is any of this relevant to what is going on? Can you manipulate the microscopic building blocks to create other universes and realities, or do you merely flow through them as though you were a tourist?"

Perculus smiled at the litany of rapid-fire questions Rebecca had rattled off. "I suppose that is the million dollar question, because if one could truly manipulate matter to such a grand scale, one would be God, which I assure you I am not. The difference between what you can perceive and what we can is a little matter of millions of years of evolution and too much time on our hands. In the end, to us it is no different than how you would view the sentient qualities of the thousands of species your kind saw fit to shepherd into extinction."

"So if your intent in showing me this is to make me feel as insignificant as a splattered bug on a windshield, you have succeeded." Though Rebecca thought she had spent most of her life questioning her perceptions in an attempt to keep her ego at bay, in reality she never had a chance. Every step forward required a belief in her ability to resolve what others could not. No ego equals no evolution.

Perculus decided to throw Rebecca a bone. "Don't take it so hard. Like you, I have spent my considerably long life following the same path. The biggest difference between you and me is that I don't die every five minutes and have to start over. Also like you, no one else has challenged me in my particular skill set."

That didn't help Rebecca. "Somehow that doesn't make any of this any easier to swallow. Also, my guess is your expanded awareness has done little to stop your kind from the same destructive qualities that we humans possess; except your disasters are on a much grander scale."

"At least we were able to stop killing each other. As far as what both Darius and Durius created to inflate their egos, the drama has been so entertaining that many didn't want to change it. However, some are beginning to see the folly in letting it continue." Though Perculus felt empathy toward the creature in front of her, she wanted to make it clear that the outcome was in question.

Rebecca took some time to chew on that before asking the obvious question. "So you don't agree that I should exist?"

"Contrary to my wishes, once we endowed your kind with a piece of us, your short lifespan kept you from evolving on your own. Slavery is slavery, no matter how benevolent the master may be. If your species is to flourish, the only answer is to allow a much longer lifespan to allow your ideas to develop. As it is now, the constant chaos of short-term solutions coupled with forgetting history inevitably leads to more destruction and chaos. Either we should give you a chance or put you out of your misery."

Rebecca shook her head in the negative. "Okay. I can buy the part where a group of higher beings decided to ramp up the abilities of some primates. However, logic dictates that after so many dilutions of that genetic material over thousands of years, the end product wouldn't have enough of that DNA left to successfully screw in a light bulb. So if I am thousands of years removed, how can you expect that if I lived for another thousand years that I can hope to come anywhere near your expanded awareness?"

Perculus thought it cute how Rebecca could so effortlessly switch to a single-minded pursuit to solve a problem. "Just because you can't understand how my spark in you could travel down such a convoluted path, doesn't mean it's not true. I can see a much younger naive version of me in you, that is, to a point. The one thing you do have that I do not is that you have absorbed some of Darius' attributes. You my dear are one of a kind."

"So I've been told. What I haven't been told is where my friends are, or if they are all right. However, I'm assuming I wouldn't be here if anything bad happened."

Rebecca put those thoughts away for the moment as she walked around the lab studying the equipment. "So what now? Are you going to explain all of this wonderful technology to me?"

"No. I'm here to watch you figure it out."

Rebecca's eyes lit up like a child in a candy store. "Seriously? Simply sit down and do what I live for?" She didn't wait for a confirmation and sat down at a work station where she recognized some of the technology, at least theoretically. "Can you teleport someone from here?"

Perculus smiled. "You tell me."

Over the next hour, Rebecca cautiously worked to interpret how the alien technology functioned, and then took small progressive steps to check her conclusions. "Are we on a spaceship or are you messing with me?"

"We are indeed in a spacecraft, though I call it home."

Rebecca felt a momentary pang of guilt that her excitement outweighed her concerns for what her friends might be going through while she experienced the thrill of a lifetime. "I think

I have this figured out. What do you have that I can send somewhere else?"

Perculus met Rebecca's request with silence, and before she could ask a second time, the lab began to disappear.

"Seriously?"

It was one thing to be stuck with Franklin for two years playing God to the Taíno, and quite another for Tony to be stuck in his home with him, the three strangers, and Renée still missing.

After a couple of hours of small talk with their guests, Tony pulled a reluctant Franklin by his arm into the kitchen again so they could be alone. "So let's see if I've got this straight. Renée and Rebecca are off on some secret mission doing god knows what, and I still don't know where Sean and Alicia are. Now you tell me the two girls in the other room are Rebecca's daughter and granddaughter. And this guy Adonis, has that ever been a real person's name since the Greek God?"

A booming voice came from the living room. "I heard that."

Tony grabbed Franklin again and rushed him into the bathroom and closed the door for more privacy.

"Is this necessary?" Franklin straightened his glasses and pulled down his coat. "I already told you there is nothing we can do but wait."

"If there's nothing to do here, why don't you send me back to the Enterprise? At least if I'm there I can help keep control of the sailors."

Franklin leaned back against the vanity. "I'm afraid that is no longer possible Tony."

Before he could question the meaning behind those words, Tony looked down to see green mist rising up his leg. "I've been meaning to ask. Why does this silly green mist shit never appear the same way?" He wasn't around long enough for Franklin to answer.

In the middle of hell, highlighted by the flames that consumed the surrounding structure, emaciated corpses piled high like cordwood covered the floor for as far as Tony could see. The overwhelming stench sent bile up his esophagus. "Auschwitz?"

"Close, Buchenwald. It is amazing the level of brutality your kind finds it necessary to inflict upon the helpless." Durius resisted the strong urge to add pieces of Tony to the piles of murdered prisoners.

Tony instantly recognized her. "You're the one who showed up at Renée's home just before everything went to hell."

"You can't blame a girl for trying."

"So that means you are Durius, the one who is trying to kill us. Is that what you are here to do? Finish the job?"

"Unfortunately, events have precluded me from harming one little hair on your grotesque head, at least this time. So can we get on with it?"

Tony, for all of his self-confidence, took a moment to steady himself before deciding to play along. "Of course, more references to Nazis. I guess I shouldn't be surprised, but it seems to me you could use a little more imagination by mixing it up with, oh I don't know, maybe some Napoleon stirred in with a pinch of Stalin and Caesar."

Despite the solemnity of the moment, Tony smiled at the contrast of the woman's peacock appearance against the horrific scene of carnage. "Wow, that is a new one, and I must say Bowie is not going to appreciate his creations upstaged by someone as evil, and I must admit, as beautiful as you."

Tony put his hands together and clapped in appreciation. "So what's your special skillset? By your over-the-top appearance, it is obvious that you don't like to dirty those beautifully manicured hands of yours. Seductress? Sorry, but I am already taken." Tony flashed his wedding ring and began to walk out of the compound.

Halfway through his second step, the burning buildings changed to a cloud of choking dust. Before Tony could protect his face, the view opened up to reveal a long trail of Native Americans slowly making their way across a desert landscape. "The only difference between the millions of Jews exterminated by the Nazis and what your white ancestors perpetrated against these people was how long it took them to die."

This time Durius sat sidesaddle atop a beautiful chestnut mare and dressed to star in a John Wayne Western. Tony rolled his eyes. "If it's all the same to you, could we skip ahead to what you want? I mean, I do understand the part where our better nature is nothing in comparison to the horrible things we do. I thought that has been firmly established."

"Don't worry Tony, I'm only showing you some of the more memorable events brought about by my hand. You need to understand this within the context of your birthright. My genetic seed is every bit a part of you as the swinging from the trees primate part is."

This wasn't a conversation Tony wanted to have. "What are you talking about? Listen lady, I am not out to solve the riddle of life or lead an army to rape and pillage. All I want is Renée back and to live out the rest of my life forgetting people like you exist." With that, Tony gave the mare a hard slap on its rear quarter, which sent the horse and rider careening down the trail. However, he didn't have long to enjoy the sight.

Back in his college dorm, a naked girl jumped out of his bed and threw Tony's wallet at him. Before he could react, words blurted out of his mouth. "You know I like you, but we agreed to see other people."

She furiously screamed, "That doesn't mean my sister could be one of them. I found her phone number in your wallet."

"But she came on to me."

A steady stream of conquests followed that showed the main course Tony majored in college, outside of football, was how to manipulate beautiful young coeds to remove their underwear. After what seemed the fiftieth encounter, he managed to regain control of his actions. "Enough. I get it. I was a complete tool in college."

Then to his dismay, Durius lay naked next to him. This time Tony was the one who jumped out of the bed.

"What's the matter lover? Can't handle a real woman?"

"As if you're a real woman." Tony grabbed a pillow off the bed and covered his private parts. "Still not getting what this has to do with anything."

"To tell you the truth, I said the same thing when I made the deal. My hope is that someone other than I agree with the obvious." Durius snapped her fingers, and they went on to the next scene.

Tony stood on a sidewalk in downtown New York with a gun drawn and aimed at a young man spread-eagled against a wall, while another office in uniform patted him down. "If this is such a waste of time, why not call it a day and return me home?"

"What do you mean, waste of time?" The officer stopped frisking the young man and turned to Tony. "This asshole needs to learn how to respect authority." With that, he took his baton off his belt and began to beat the suspect to the ground.

"What are you doing?" Tony holstered his weapon to grab his partner's baton.

"The only joy I get out of you miserable parasites is when you beat the shit out of each other for the sheer joy of it." Durius watched as a crowd began to gather around a site never witnessed before. One cop stepping outside of the Blue Wall of Silence to stop a case of excessive force.

Unfortunately for Tony, while he tried to pin his partner to the ground, the young man, instead of running away, reached down and pulled Tony's gun from its holster.

Before either officer could react, four shots rang out sending the potential killer flying back against the wall. They both turned to see Durius blowing the smoke from the barrel of a gun. "I guess you can say that this is a perfect case of two wrongs making a right."

Sitting up, Tony shook his head in disbelief. "You knew this was going to happen?"

Durius gave Tony a look that said, *duh*. "Makes you wonder who it is you feel so honor bound to protect, doesn't it?"

The abusive officer disappeared, followed by the rest of the urban environment. Next, a searing heat hit Tony that made breathing difficult. Shielding his eyes from the bright sunlight, he could make out a large crowd of men shrouded in white robes and the trademark Gutra headgear worn throughout the Arab world. Kneeling in the center of a large plaza were three men with their hands tied behind their back.

"It looks as though these boys' day is not going to end well. Oh look, here comes the ax man."

A large man approached them and cleaved all three heads clean off with his sword in the space of a minute. Tony turned away as the heads bounced off the paved surface and rolled away.

"Yeah, so what else is new?"

"Exactly, what else is new? He chopped the heads off those young men because they had the audacity to tweet their support for women to drive in Saudi Arabia. Yet you spent how many months in the Gulf of Hormuz defending their leader's right to do exactly the same type of violence against their own citizens as their enemies do?"

This was a sore spot for Tony. "Are you asking me if I think it was right? No, it wasn't, but what you want to know is how can I claim the moral high ground when there isn't any?"

"So maybe this wasn't such a waste of time." Durius snapped her fingers and they appeared on a hill overlooking the I-405 Freeway in the Sepulveda Pass between the San Fernando Valley and West Los Angeles. As usual, thousands of cars and trucks sat in gridlock with engines running. "A perfect microcosm of humanity, going nowhere in a hurry as they despoil the environment they need to keep them alive.

"My question to you Captain Anthony Knox is if almost all of your fellow human beings are so miserable, why wouldn't any rational entity think it would be doing the universe a favor to make all of them disappear?"

Tony stood wordless for a moment as he watched the insanity below. "Work during the week to live on the weekend, the story of modern life. Do I believe there is any hope? Apparently more than you."

As he continued, Tony turned away from the traffic below. "Mankind is pedal to the metal headed for the next Dark Ages. Only an idiot, and unfortunately there are far too many of them, can't fathom the inevitability of a complete societal collapse. Does that mean the end of man? No – just the next opportunity to get it right.

"If you take into account all that I have learned since that day off the California coast when we transported into 1941, I would have to amend my beliefs. Now I would say that only when one can remove one's personal hubris and billions of others simply disappear will human life be worth living."

Durius couldn't stand the toxic brew the cars below created, so a snap of the fingers took them high up in the beautiful Sierra Nevada mountain range, where she took a deep breath. "That was quite a mouthful coming from someone who has seen the worst. You want to put the blame on everything but those who are right in front of you. Sounds like a Disney fairy tale, though I lean more toward The Walking Dead point of view."

Tony had to admit there was more to agree with Durius' position than disagree with. "I hope that world we managed to clean up will have the time it needs to evolve into something better. Oh, and the answer to one of your earlier questions is in that world no one will be afraid to tell the truth or follow an immoral religious leader bent on forcing their god's will down everyone's throat."

Tony leaned down, picked up a small stone, and threw it lazily against a tree. "One last thing before I hope you leave. You said that your seed is a part of who I am. If that is the case, I have to say, for all of the shit you have been throwing down, there must be an incredible entity underneath all of your rage. Good luck dealing with it. It might be nice to get to know your good side when you are done hating on us."

For a moment, Durius went back to the times before Darius' indiscretion changed everything and remembered her earlier encounters with those who followed her lineage. For a split second, she saw Tony in this light, and it almost brought a smile to her jaded face – almost.

Then she returned to reality. "I'm sure throughout your life you have questioned why it is that you were given such a short lifespan. I will tell you that it wasn't my idea, and if you have the opportunity to run into your Carl Eddington again, you might want to ask him whose it was."

⤜⬦⤛

Suddenly, Tony was back at his home standing in front of a smiling Franklin, who reached out and pinched his cheeks. Tony pushed his hand away. "Why did you do that?"

"I wanted to make sure it was genuinely you."

Tony looked around the room to see they were alone. "Of course it's me, you horse's ass. Where did the others go? Do they get a go at her now?"

"I'm simply shocked you came back in one piece. Don't get me wrong, I am extremely pleased to see you so, but Durius isn't exactly known for her restraint." Franklin handed Tony one of the glasses of French wine that appeared in his hands. "Regarding Phoenix, her daughter Lydia, and Adonis, I have set them up in a nice little place near the outskirts of Havana. I figured they might want to see some of the sights while they waited."

"So, what was that all about?"

Franklin once again had to think about how much to let Tony know. "You had an audience with Durius while she was honor bound to only judge you."

"She told me I am a direct descendant of hers."

"And then there's that." Franklin was surprised she would give Tony this information.

Tony wanted to get a rise out of him. "So what does that make me, a demigod?"

Franklin drained his glass and laughed at the idea. "No, simply human I'm afraid."

Then before he could say another word, Tony was once again gone. "It's starting to look like whack-a-mole around here," Franklin grumbled. "What the heck, I might as well go see how the others are settling in."

Then he too disappeared, leaving the house empty, or so he thought as a shadowy figure walked silently through the front door. After searching the whole house and finding no one, Aaron threw up his arms in surrender. "Great, *mother*," he complained, "You sent me to the wrong place." Frustrated, he slammed the door on his way out.

When the scene changed, Alicia still sat on the edge of a bed, but this time it was simple, firm, and the covers stretched across it so tight you could bounce a quarter off of it. "The Academy?"

"Yes the Naval Academy, circa 1979, home to one of the last bastions of gender harassment. Green dye in your shower water an hour before inspection, uniforms dyed pink, instructors constantly singling you out for imaginary deficiencies, six attempted sexual assaults, and all in your plebe year. Yes the good old days." Surius was kind enough to stop there.

In checking out her uniform, Alicia could tell another of the demeaning trivial tasks meted out by her sadistic superior, midshipman second-class Wally *Bubba* Platt, was on her schedule today.

"Why are you still sitting with your finger up your ass when I ordered you to scrub down the head?"

"Right on time," Alicia thought as her body involuntarily tightened. "Yes Sir, no excuses." Once again, she was without any control over her reactions. All she could do was live with the rage buried barely under the surface. The rage intensified when she opened the door to the bathroom to see two upper class cadets against the far wall, while two others sat on the sinks. "It's about time midshipman fourth-class *Alicia* Calhoun."

Alicia found her way blocked by Bubba when she tried to back away from the threat. "I don't want any trouble." Having gone through this six times previously, Alicia backed into a corner, dropped to the floor, and put her arms and hands in front of her body and face in a defensive position.

The five cadets closed in and made a semicircle around her. "Oh, it's no trouble cadet. We want to know for sure if you are a dyke or not." Bubba leaned down and tried to stroke her hair.

Alicia waited until he reached the top of her head before she violently grabbed his arm and dug her nails as hard as she could into his flesh. His impulse to pull away ensured that she had left four 3-inch long gashes.

"You fucking bitch," he screamed as he used his backhand to try to smack Alicia across the face. Fortunately, her training paid off as he caused himself more pain than her when he connected instead with the boney side of her forearm.

Before she could change to a better defensive position, the pack lifted her struggling body off the floor, pinned her to the wall, and began to rip off her uniform.

Alicia realized it would be seconds before they got her completely naked and fought them as hard as she could.

What happened next changed her cynical outlook that all men

were pigs.

"What are you cadets doing!"

Alicia opened her eyes to see an enraged midshipman first-class grab the closest cadet attacking her by his neck and throw him hard into one of the sinks.

Entangled in the tight quarters during their assault on Alicia, the other three cadets could offer no help to the second of Alicia's attackers, who happened to be Bubba. With him, Alicia's savior didn't hold back as he punched him several times in the face rendering him too stunned to respond. As a final indignity, her savior brought up his knee with as much force as he could muster into Bubba's groin.

Outside on the parade ground, cadets stopped at the sound of his screams.

By this time the other three managed to free themselves and were about to charge their tormentor. However, they stopped short when they caught sight of three burly cadets behind Alicia's rescuer.

"You got this?" one of them asked.

With a look that said, *bring it on*, he faced the three now standing above Alicia. "You losers want me to continue, or are you ready to go back to your quarters to wait for charges?"

Seeing the other three waiting their turn to pummel them, they cautiously made their way toward the exit.

"Pick up the trash before you leave," he ordered.

After they struggled to retrieve their injured companions, they cowered as they made their way around the cadets who still had their arms cocked back ready to attack.

As his friends followed the attackers away from the scene, he slowly approached Alicia, as she attempted with trembling hands to restore her modesty. He turned away and stood guard at the door to allow Alicia time to cover up the best she could with the ripped uniform. "I'll wait outside until you pull yourself together, or I can wait here if you need me to."

With tears streaming down her bruised face, she kneeled down on the floor. Though she was in a state of shock, Alicia had regained enough of her senses to ask, "Why did you help me? I thought you all hated me."

You are supposed to be our sister-in-arms, and if we don't have our sister's back, what kind of brothers would we be?"

His inner calm and kindness brought a smile to her troubled face. "What's your name, Sir?"

"Midshipman First-Class Sean Phillips at your service, cadet."

As she looked up at her handsome hero, Admiral Alicia Calhoun, shed a few tears reliving the moment she first meet her future husband. Then reality stepped back in as she listened to her younger self. "Sir, as much as I appreciate you saving me, I humbly request that you drop any idea of charging those assholes with what happened here. I have enough trouble with my instructors as it is than to add bringing charges that, based on my and other female cadets' past experiences with the senior officers, will only put me on trial instead."

Looking down at her, Sean could tell this determined plebe deserved better. "All right. As a senior, I control what goes on around here within the student ranks. So I will instead put the word out that you and your brave sister cadets are off limits to any form of hazing by their fellow Neanderthals. Will that suffice?"

Alicia accepted his offered hand to help her up. "That would be great, Sir."

Sean grabbed a towel, wetted it, and handed it to her.

She smiled at Sean as she straightened her hair, tucked in her shirt, and used the wet towel to wipe the scrapes that covered her arms and face.

Alicia remembered with fondness how Sean lived up to his promise repeatedly. He always managed to show up whether it was another cadet trying to grope her, or an overly insistent academy officer pinning her in a corner after class. Over the years, they both had joked how his empathy for her put two strikes against him with his senior officers. However, he never took the idea seriously.

As Alicia reminisced about how Sean gave her the tools that she passed on to the underclass female cadets who followed, Surius changed the scene again. "I bet you know where you're headed next."

Seated on the edge of her bed, she brushed her dress shoes to a polished finish. "Graduation day? Six hours of pomp and circumstance that sucks the life out of you, followed by Bubba who tried one last time to finish what he started?"

"Yeah, but the manner you dealt with him this time had a far more favorable outcome."

Alicia chuckled at the memory. "I don't need to see the sight of Bubba writhing on the ground holding his broken man bits in his hands again."

"Nor do you need to see how many women over the ensuing years had you to thank for saving them from the same abuses. Where Sean's career never reached the potential of his talents because of this sense of a higher purpose, yours benefited greatly when it came time to trot you out as an example of how far the Navy had come toward gender equality. Wasn't this why you choose to leave sea duty behind and enter into the political side?"

"It was the only way I could think of to study the enemy at home."

"And here you and Sean are now. All because of your relentless refusal to accept the status quo you found so corrupt." Surius surprised Alicia when she reached out and gave her a hug.

Alicia briefly reciprocated before she pulled away. "Does this mean we are done?"

"Only if you're not interested in where you began." Surius said this in a way to suggest to Alicia that she should agree. "Don't worry. Sean and the rest of the gang are fine. I can safely say overall they are enjoying their experiences." He then hesitated before he added, "Except maybe your mate."

"Except for my mate? What after tearing up his mind into a billion pieces, are you guys having trouble putting him back together again?" Alicia didn't mean to come off so flippant about the love of her life, but this was the point of reference she had from their last time together.

Surius laughed at the idea. "We'd have more trouble trying to figure out how to do that with one of your primitive rockets. No, his problem stems from one of your culture's old adages: *With great power comes great responsibility*. For the moment, he can't make up his mind about what that means. Then again, based on how long it took for him to finally mate with you, we all may have a lot of free time on our hands."

Alicia rose to Sean's defense. "That wasn't only on him. In our own ways, we both understood my career would go nowhere if I were in a relationship with senior brass. It simply isn't done."

"Yeah, whatever," Surius shrugged. "Let's play a new game, and this time, why don't I let you chose where we play it."

A vision flashed through Alicia's mind, and before she could react to it, they were off again. Her academy dorm room disappeared, and the front of early 20th century American mansion stood in its place. Alicia looked around, and the first thing to grab her attention was the black 1959 Cadillac hearse parked in the driveway. Before she could put it together, the sound of the large front double doors opening caused her to turn around. Silhouetted in the large doorframe stood a diminutive young man dressed in a black suit, a scowl firmly affixed to his face. "Oh my god. That's Harold."

Surius got a kick out of how Alicia sounded like a teenager. "Check your pocket."

Alicia put her hand in her jacket pocket and pulled out a mirror, which she put in front of her face to see the 82-year-old Ruth Gordon staring back at her. "Harold and Maude, one of the greatest movies ever made. Though for your sake this look better not be permanent."

"I figured why not let you spend time as the woman who was the first to show you how much power you had when you ignored acceptable norms and instead held true to your inner voice. So, what will it be first? To the graveyard, stealing the policeman's motorcycle, or blowing bubbles after sex?"

"Let's start with the graveyard, and see how it goes from there." The idea of having sex with a teenager, especially in her current form horrified Alicia.

All the time Alicia conversed with Surius in her head, Harold stood still staring at her. "Fortunately, this would be considered normal behavior to him."

"So what are you waiting for? I haven't got all day." To Alicia's amazement, her voice had the same deep, raspy inflections she remembered loving so well coming out of Ruth Gordon's mouth.

Harold bounded down the stairs and rushed to open the large car's front passenger door with a flourish. "Your chariot awaits."

The instant Alicia sat on the overstuffed leather seat she felt herself drifting into the memory. For the next three hours, Alicia lived in a long lost world where for the first time in her young life the world made sense. She could not imagine a better way to spend the day.

⟨⟩

After Sean licked the last chilidog wrapper clean, he got up off the recliner and stretched as he wondered, "What would I do if I was the last person on Earth, and I had the ability to build whatever I want from scratch?"

"I don't know about you, but I would build one of the galaxy's largest arenas and fill it with adoring fans."

To find that he was happy to hear Bowie's voice surprised Sean. "Regardless of my lack of performing skills? That would be some trick. Why are you here?"

"I was in the neighborhood and heard you could use some company. How about creating your own new species and teach them to worship you as their god."

As Bowie talked, a grand Cathedral in the Gothic style arose around them. Sean stared at a giant statue modeled after him mounted behind the strangest looking altar he could imagine. Instead of candles, golden chalices, and refined tapestry on the raised platform, a lush forest stood instead. "Here we go with the Cathedral theme again. So what's the message? Love thy tree as you would love your rose?"

"At least the trees wouldn't put a crown of thorns on your head and nail you to a cross."

As they walked toward the altar, he noticed the seats fill with worshipers. As they compared him to the man carved in stone behind the altar, the cavernous space began to hum with excited whispers.

Sean stopped so short, Bowie bumped into him, causing their god to stumble before collecting himself. A collective sigh reverberated throughout the Cathedral. Sean slowly regained his balance. "I have a feeling this is going to get uncomfortable real quick."

"Trust me, you can get used to screaming fans trying to rip your clothes off."

No sooner had Bowie said this, than a few of the congregation on both sides of the aisle ventured cautiously from the pews and slowly approached. This was all it took for the rest of the three thousand worshipers to push forward in a wave. In a matter of seconds, a sea of humanity surrounded Sean and threatened to crush him. With one panicked thought, the whole scene disappeared, replaced with the same high mountain scenery as before.

"That must be how the Beatles felt in 1964."

Sean smiled at Bowie's remark. "Makes you wonder why the real Bowie never got that big; he must not have wanted it. In these mad times, why can't we be outrageous? I mean, when was the last time elephants came from miles away to congregate for the festival of singing pop-loving pachyderms."

As he said this the ground shook from the weight of twenty elephants as they sang, *"I'm thinking of good vibrations, she's giving me good citations."*

Sean laughed with joy. "Twenty part harmony, yes!"

Then the elephants disappeared and the scene shifted to a sandy beach with a row of B&Bs lining its edge. "No surprise there."

His heart sunk as he looked out of the window at the view he and Alicia had enjoyed while on their honeymoon in Cambria.

Bowie shook his head in bewilderment. "The fate of humanity rests on the shoulders of a person more suited to be a Jesuit than revolutionary. Franklin eats this shit up. But no, instead of me working with Tony, who would have his world up and humming, and sipping a Mai Tai on a beach by now, I am stuck with you. You on the other hand wish to debate the meaning of creation. After all that you have seen over 155 years, do you actually think you might have missed something? I mean it's not as if we're on a clock or anything, but for the love of my sanity could you put away all of the esoteric bullshit and do something?"

Sean smiled an evil grin and did just that. Not a trace of the usual green mist marked where Bowie had vanished. "Okay, so there are advantages to being a god."

⸻❖⸻

Captain Daniel Osaka woke up to find someone violently shaking him. "All right. I'm awake already." When he rolled over to find out who had so rudely interrupted his sleep, Daniel was shocked to see Renée standing over him. "Why…"

She didn't wait for him to finish. "No, I don't know why either one of us are here, or where here is."

Renée surveyed the room. "Let's see, rough wood floor, stucco walls, six-shooters in leather holsters on the coatrack, and folded jeans with a plaid shirt for you on the oversized brass bed. Looks like the late 19th Century American West."

Renée walked over and removed one of the Colt 45 Peacemakers from its holster. "You know these are here for a reason, and that reason can't mean anything good for us. You ever use one of these?"

When Renée spun the cylinder on the Colt, Osaka understood the implications of the question and jumped out of bed. Fortunately, he wore long johns complete with the buttoned back door. "The only side arm I've trained with is the 9mm Glock 19."

Daniel talked as he dressed. "I was with a little girl who turned into a flower dragon, after which I fell asleep and woke up here. What about you?"

"Mine was female as well. She told me that those who have pulled us down this rabbit hole will judge us to determine if humanity should continue to exist."

Renée opened the door of the room to confirm that indeed they were in a Western hotel right out of a 1950s TV Western. At the end of the hall, she noticed movement behind the stairway banister. She casually backed into the room and quietly shut the door. "We've got to move."

She looked out the window to learn they were in luck, if they hurried. "It's only a two floor drop down to an alley below."

As he tucked in his shirt, Osaka asked, "What about my ship and crew? Did they sink into that weird landscape, or did I dream it all?"

"I don't know what happened to anyone else, but if I had to hazard a guess, I'd say if it was bad, it was real." Renée strapped her holster on and tied the hanging leather strips around her leg. "Let's talk about that later."

She then threw the other gun and holster to Osaka. "Put this on." Renée put a foot out the window while grabbing the ledge and slowly lowered herself until the only thing Daniel could see were her hands, until those too disappeared.

He looked out to see she had landed safely, and after taking too long to strap on his holster, he followed. No sooner had he let go, than the door to the room burst open.

Renée grabbed Osaka's hand and jerked him to his feet. "This way!"

As they reached the end of the alley, two riders on horses appeared to cut them off. When they turned to run back in the other direction two cowboy-hatted heads popped out of the window. Renée's Colt was out and aimed before Osaka had time to comprehend their limited options.

"Cover me!" she yelled as she pulled the hammer back and discharged two rounds into the wall next to the window. As the two heads disappeared into the room, she whipped around and to her amazement recognized Kalius. "You've got to be kidding me."

Osaka was about to fire at the two riders, when Renée yelled, "Cease fire!"

Kalius motioned to them to hurry.

As they ran toward the two riders, they discovered two saddled horses in tow.

Before they could mount properly, bullets landed all around them, which sent their mounts forward in a panic. As they raced down the dirt street, Renée reached out to steady Osaka before he fell off his out-of-control steed. When sure that he would stay in the saddle, Renée looked ahead to see the townsfolk scramble to get clear of their stampeding horses.

It took only a minute to clear the last building before open country lay ahead. As they passed under it, Renée glanced back to read the name painted on the sign that hung above the road. "Damn. Tombstone. I don't remember any females involved in the fighting."

When they were five miles outside of town and could tell no one had followed, Kalius pulled in the reigns on her horse. The others followed suit. "Who's to say the same is true here? You did notice those back there tried to kill you. Believe me, they weren't gunning for Daniel."

Jesus leaned to his left and spit. "Kalius has always been peeved that in none of the Darius and Durius worlds were there any female versions of that man always on top thing. The women of your species have proven to be every bit as ruthless as their counterparts."

Osaka didn't like the sound of that. "So what does that make me, the damsel in distress?"

Kalius pointed to Renée. "Which makes you Wyatt Earp, and you just ran out on a town full of people counting on you."

"Jesus Christ! And I suppose not one of those townsfolk the story says I have to rescue is willing to stand with me." Renée then turned and faced Jesus with a confused look on her face. "And who are you supposed to be?"

Kalius was quick to answer. "You already said it. Jesus Christ."

"Yeah, it's me. I didn't feel my first test for Daniel here challenged him enough, so I enlisted help from Kalius who in her infinite wisdom helped set up this little soirée."

Osaka could not come to terms with the incongruity of Jesus on top of a horse dressed in full cowboy gear that included the spurs on his boot heels. "So you were the one behind the little girl who turned into a flower dragon. What was that about?"

Jesus ignored Daniel's question. "This is a moral dilemma for Renée to work out, and a chance for me to see if your inner calmness holds up with the shoe on the other foot. Win, win."

Renée got it, sort of. "So, either we go back to Tombstone and get drilled with a bunch of bullet holes or we keep riding away and all of humanity perishes. And what you said about Captain Osaka, I haven't got a clue what any of that means. Anything else we should know before you two leave?"

Kalius addressed Jesus. "I told you she was a smart girl." Then to Renée's question, she added, "Only that you are already a legend in your own time with the way you handle a six-shooter, and that Osaka's reputation as the most successful madam in the West sold millions of ten cent novels."

This whole set up horrified Osaka. "What am I supposed to do? And excuse me, but you sure don't act like any son of God I ever imagined."

Jesus laughed. "What can I say? I am a complicated savior. Besides, it's not like you have anything to fear. No one in town wants to hurt you – yet."

With that final thought, Jesus put spurs to his horse and pulled back on the reins, which caused it to rear up. "Hi-ho Silver! Away!"

"He's always wanted to do that," Kalius shouted, as they galloped away to vanish after they had cleared a hundred yards.

Renée shook her head sympathetically. "I don't blame you if you decide not to play along. However, if I have learned anything over the last five hundred years, it is that inaction also leads to consequences. The difference is you no longer have any control over the outcome."

Osaka struggled for a moment with the implications of his situation. "So we are in a world where the female dominates, but I'm a strong male where men are not empowered. Then to top it all off, how we handle the situation plays into whether or not humanity keeps breathing?"

It was Renée's turn to figure out how much to share of what she knew. "Screw it," she thought. "When you left Cuba with the entire Enterprise Task Force and crew, I was the only one left behind. Believe it or not, I lived through the next four hundred years, and you know what I learned from being alive so long?"

"Four hundred years?" The idea was too incredible to believe.

"Not the point. Try to stay focused, Captain."

"Sorry, please continue."

"What I learned was the complete transitory nature of a human life. It didn't matter how important, smart, or successful you were, because within one hundred years after the end of your short life, you are forgotten to time. After a couple hundred years, you learn this also holds true in matters of your own perspective. Personally speaking, the only time I can learn anything anymore is if my entire world turns upside down and I'm forced into reactive thinking."

Osaka wasn't buying all of it. "In the cerebral sense, I can follow that, but I don't understand how matters such as your relationship with Tony and the rest of us whose experiences laid the foundation for all that came afterward wouldn't still be important. We are still here, and I don't believe after four hundred years those formative experiences mean any less today than all of those years ago."

Osaka's words caught Renée by surprise, and before she could suppress her emotions, tears began to roll down her face. "I didn't say being separated from all of those I loved and cared about didn't color every one of my choices. If you expect life to reward you for every correct decision, you will always be disappointed. The game is rigged in favor of those with the ability to forget and move on."

Daniel felt for Renée. "Yet, after four hundred years of trying you are still unable to do that."

Osaka had learned enough to decide what he should do. "For me, I guess it is time to find out how enlightened I am. You got a plan for all this that won't get us killed in the process?"

Renée turned her horse back toward town. "I guess that all depends on whether or not your whore house has what I'll need to neutralize the ones who want to kill me. If not, hey, who wants to live forever anyway?"

"Ah yes, spoken by the one who has lived for half a millennium. Personally, I'd prefer to get back to my family and last at least another fifty," Osaka answered, as he swung his horse around.

As they walked their horses back to Tombstone, the town silhouetted against the setting Sun.

———◦———

According to the clothes she wore and the cars driving down the busy neon lit boulevard with shades of grey and black, Rebecca realized this was 1930s Los Angeles film noir. "What's a classy dame like you doing in a reality like this?"

She recognized Tony's voice, and turned to see him leaning against the wall in the entryway to a seedy motel. When he stepped out of the shadows, Rebecca had to stifle a laugh at the costume he wore. The grey Fedora rakishly tilted over his left eye and the wide lapelled suit he wore was all way out of character. "How long have you been standing there, and who in the world dressed you up like Dick Powell?"

He gave her a hug, and stepped back. "You should talk. How can you walk in that dress? And what about the veil on that pillbox hat of yours?"

The dress was actually a skirt with three inch spiked heels that fit tightly to the curves of her body all the way down the length of her legs. To complete the look, an open matching grey waistcoat revealed a buttoned up ruffled white blouse set off by the bright red lipstick and pancake makeup.

"You are right about one thing. I can't move. Could you please reach down and take off these ridiculous shoes before I kill myself?"

When Tony tried to oblige, he found it necessary to lie down on the pavement to do so. Rebecca made matters worse when she tried to remove the hat that to her dismay had a hundred pins holding it to her head. Physics took over from there with her falling on top of Tony, he with one of her shoes in one hand, the other keeping her head from striking the pavement. After a moment to assess nothing too severely damaged but their pride, they both burst out laughing.

So consumed with the silliness of this new situation, neither noticed the black sedan that pulled a U-turn right in front of them; the passenger door opened as it stopped. "Are you two out of your fricking minds? You're going to get us all killed. Get in before all of Los Angeles knows we're here."

Rebecca and Tony both looked at the diminutive man holding the door and the burly driver, and then back at each other.

"You think we're supposed to go somewhere with them?" Rebecca asked.

"I don't know. You know I'm not known for making rational life decisions for myself." This elicited another round of laughter as Tony struggled to get Rebecca back on her feet.

"What is wrong with you two idiots?" The diminutive man jumped out of the car and rushed over to help Tony to his feet. When they got a good look at him, the laughter intensified. Straw Bowler hat, blue bow tie with red polka dots, and a suit every bit as garish to match embellished his short rotund bowling ball body.

"Listen dumbshits. If Casey finds out you have been fooling around without the job being done, we're all dead. Come on and get in the fricking car."

They both finally heard the desperation in their newfound friend's voice and hustled to comply.

"So where are we headed?" Tony asked this of the stone-faced man who sat behind the wheel.

"That depends if you two got what you needed from Rusty. Did you?"

Tony realized things could get sticky if they did not answer in the affirmative, but struggled to come up with a plausible excuse. "Well, you know how difficult Rusty can be." He looked at Rebecca with a shrug that said, *That's all I've got, how about you?*

"You've got to be kidding. You know what happens to us if we come back empty handed? The deal is you bring us the name, and we tell you where we have the Oswald's little brat stashed away." The colorfully dressed little man leaned so far over the passenger seat, Tony felt the spray of his saliva strike his face.

While this went on, something uncomfortable under the layers of clothes that covered her chest made Rebecca squirm in her seat. She turned away to unbutton her blouse enough to retrieve the offending article scratching her breast.

She stealthily read what was on the scrap of paper before she turned to face Tony. "That's okay lover. You can stop stalling."

Then, with a look that she hoped conveyed menace, demanded, "You will get the name after you take us to the kid." Then for dramatic effect, she stuffed the note back down her bra.

"I always knew you were the brains of the outfit, Nora." Satisfied, he turned back to face front. "We still have to see the boss first."

Rebecca looked at Tony, and silently mouthed. "That can't be good."

"You got anything else down there that might help?"

Rebecca playfully slugged Tony in the arm. "Nothing you need to see." Pretending to look out the window, she removed the paper and handed it to Tony. "It looks like a land deed."

Tony looked at it, and his eyes went wide. "The name on it is David Graham. This means you are Nora, I'm Nick Charles, and the droll little guy in the front seat is Joe Morelli. We are in *The Thin Man* movie!"

Rebecca turned to look at Tony. "The problem with that is I appear to be twenty years too late. Besides, this car would be loaded with alcohol if it were."

With his attention directed out of the rear window, Tony was only half listening to her. "I think we are being followed."

Joe whipped around to see another black sedan with its headlights off about half a block behind them and smacked the driver on the shoulder. "Step on it and lose them!"

As soon as their car sped up, a siren began to scream in the night air and the chase was on. This being decades before seatbelts, after one particularly violent turn Rebecca slammed into his body, which threw Tony face first into the window. When the car straightened out, it was his turn to fall onto Rebecca. The car lurched again as it went wide into a turn. The driver over-corrected, which sent the car into a spin. When it finally came to a stop, buried on the driver's side floorboard, Joe Morelli's body had pinned the driver's legs in place.

When Tony turned to see Rebecca halfway out of the car, he rapidly exited on his side.

A 1969 Plymouth Belvedere painted in LAPD black and white slid to a stop alongside, and two officers promptly exited with guns drawn. The driver addressed Tony, who was in complete disbelief. "Glad to see you and the little lady are okay, Mr. Charles."

"So are we Officer Malloy." Tony stared with amazement at the star of *Adam 12*, a police procedural series that ran on TV until 1975.

On the other side of the car, Rebecca forgot about her restrictive dress and once again fell flat on her back. Before she could gather herself, the driver managed to extract himself and aimed his gun at her.

Rebecca threw her hands over her face and waited for the shot that never came. To her surprise, Malloy's partner Jim Reed had aimed a strange little rectangular box at the armed driver who now lay unconscious on the ground three feet from her.

Once again, Rebecca could not keep from cracking up. Joe's face peeking out from the floorboards only made it worse. "Really, a phaser set to stun?"

By the time Tony reached Rebecca, Officer Reed had helped her to her feet, but as she began to disappear, he wound up falling back against the police car. He looked over to see Tony shrug as he too disappeared in a puff of green mist.

As she watched all of this play out, Perculus found herself in the same state of mind. "How could you not want to keep them around? With their imagination and ability to adapt on demand, the possibilities are endless. *Tis to laugh*, as one extremely intelligent bunny once observed."

When she didn't respond, Perculus realized Durius' mind was

somewhere else. "Planet Earth to Durius." She then laughed at her bad pun.

Durius hadn't heard from Aaron and had let his lack of action consume her. "What are you prattling on about? If I wanted entertainment, we both know of a thousand other worlds where the inhabitants can not only put on a show, but also offer it across multiple dimensions. You've had your fun, now let's see how they do when we expose their more primal nature."

Phoenix and Adonis were finishing a late breakfast at a little sidewalk café overlooking a beautiful plaza in downtown Havana.

"It's a shame Lydia didn't want to join us," Adonis sighed. "She would have gotten a kick out of that three-dimensional game shop across the street."

"Yeah, that's what a teenage girl who got ripped out of her comfort zone wants to do, spend the day with the mom she feels responsible for her turmoil." Phoenix finished off her Bloody Mary and motioned with the empty glass to the server for a refill, then thought better of it. "We should get back."

"We've been stuck in that house since we were deposited here over a week ago. Granted, it is one hell of a house in the way Franklin wired it to automatically provide whatever you want, but we needed to get out."

Adonis got the server's attention and stuck up two fingers. "Besides, according to the news the house displays every two hours, there is no such thing as crime. You've got nothing to worry about, so enjoy it why you can."

Phoenix sighed. Worrying about her 16-year-old daughter's feelings wasn't the only issue she thought about. "Why isn't Sean Anthony here? Or better yet, why hasn't he told me what's going on?"

"Probably for the same reasons your father-in-law kept Sean Anthony's mother in the dark. They're playing on a different playing field than us, and let me tell you man, we're Pop Warner to their NFL."

Right on cue, the drinks arrived. Adonis admired how the server was always in the right place at the right time. "I can get used to this place."

Lydia always knew her family was different. Though there were many differences from the world she grew up in than the one of her mother, social media wasn't one of them. Unfortunately for her, this Cuba didn't evolve in quite the same way.

"This sucks. No Facebook, no Google, no YouTube, no Twitter, no Instagram, only this stupid hologram that wants to know why I'm so unhappy."

Then addressing the hologram, she asked, "You really want to know? I'm bored, all of my friends are gone, and I'm stuck here in the middle of nowhere. You got anything for that?"

The young female holograph behind her offered a solution. "If you go for a brisk walk, your increased heart rate can help your body release endorphins that increase brain activity. It might give you a healthier outlook on your new environment."

Lydia picked up one of the couch pillows and threw it through the image, then plopped down on the couch and put another one over her head while kicking her legs in frustration. "That's it. I'm in hell. I should have gone into Havana with Mom and Uncle Adonis. "

"There is someone approaching the front door."

Lydia peaked back at the hologram with a sneer. Then in a flash of enthusiasm, she sprung from the couch, hoping it would be her father. After she threw the door open, her smile vanished when confronted by the male stranger who stood on the porch. "Who are you?"

"Let's leave it at, I'm your long lost uncle, so you'll feel a little less panicked about where we're going."

Something in the way he said this, sent chills running up Lydia's spine. "Like hell I'm going anywhere with you." She turned to flee, when she noticed the green mist creep up her legs. "Crap."

Aaron looked around the room and noticed the hologram. "You might want to inform the kid's parents she won't be home for dinner."

"I'm not afraid of you." Lydia was definitely afraid of the man who had kidnapped her. She glanced around to see the room they occupied was similar to one of those old movies her grandmother liked to watch. The sheet metal walls, rows of tires on the wall, tools scattered all over, and the early 20th Century car parked on the rails of a lift identified it as an old service bay at a gas station. "When my mom and dad find you they are going to kick your ass."

Aaron saw through the teenager. "If I were you, I'd be more worried about what I can do to you." He brought his face within inches of hers, and licked his lips. "So behave yourself while your uncle goes to have a little chat with your daddy."

"Uncle?" Lydia's question came too late as Aaron vanished. "Why didn't anybody tell me Dad had a madman for a brother?"

When she couldn't find a comfortable place to sit down, Lydia cautiously walked over to open the single door next to the overhead garage door and peeked out. With a fright, she violently slammed the door. "Holy shit!"

⚬⟡⚬

By the time Renée and Osaka reached the outskirts of Tombstone, the sky was almost black.

"So what direction do you think we should pick." Because Renée had long outranked him, the subservient part of Osaka's 19th Century female role came natural.

Renée stood tall in the saddle as she scanned the darkness. "It seems to me that building with the bell tower might be a good place to start." She removed her gun, replaced the two spent bullets, and holstered it.

"I suppose the priest won't be happy to see me," Daniel worried.

Renée laughed. "What do you mean? If it's anything similar to a modern church, she's probably one of your biggest clients."

"She?" Osaka didn't need to wait for her to explain. "Of course it's a she."

Fortunately, the church lay at the edge of town. They rode to the back of the building, dismounted, and tied their horses to the hitch. As they quietly opened the door and stepped inside, they came face to face with a middle-aged woman who wore a white collar on a black blouse.

"What are you doing here?" the stunned preacher protested.

Renée thought about how she should properly address her. "We're sorry Pastor, but if you wouldn't mind, could you please tell us where the killers are, and we'll be on our way."

The preacher walked past Osaka to scan the street. When she found it empty, she quietly shut it. "For all that you are trying to do to save the town, I will tell you anything I know that can be of help, but *he* will have to wait here." She motioned to Renée to follow before she turned to head over to the simple wooden seats.

"Really?" Osaka liked his role less by the second.

Renée tried to calm the nervous preacher. "I respect your discomfort over my friend's presence here, so I'll make it brief. Who hired the gunslingers to kill me?"

Now the cleric was confused. "You know as well as I that the only person with a reason is Barlow."

Her answer didn't help. "Why don't we start with your name. Then you can tell me what Barlow has to gain by my death."

The preacher looked at Renée as though she had lost her mind, but complied. "My name is Pastor Elizabeth. That evil bitch rancher Barlow isn't satisfied with owning all of the water rights in the north end of the valley, so she now wants the rest of the water rights. She had her gunslingers try to murder the only landowner in the valley big enough to stand up to her. Everyone in town knows you have her tucked away somewhere safe, so when you ask why you are important to Barlow, that's why."

Now that Renée knew the situation, she remembered something along similar lines in a Western she watched as a kid that gave her an idea. "Do you know where this Barlow is now?"

Pastor Elizabeth shook her head. "As soon as you escaped, he and his killers went to your friend's sin palace. They plan to look for Henderson tomorrow."

Renée felt she had enough information. "Thank you for your time Pastor Elizabeth. If you don't mind me sticking around for a little while longer after I send my friend away, I would appreciate it."

The churchwoman thought about the risk before she meekly agreed. "As long as he takes both horses with him when he goes. I can't have it found out I am harboring you here. They wouldn't give a second thought to burning down the church with both of us still in it."

Renée nodded in agreement. "Wait here."

She then walked over to where Daniel waited by the back door. There she relayed the information and the plan to defuse the situation to an increasingly nervous Osaka. "I need you to go to your brothel."

"You want me to go into a room full of hired killers and get them shitfaced so you can grab this Barlow woman?" Then Osaka realized a major problem with this scenario. "What if one of them decides they want me instead of one of my boys?"

"I guess you'll have to learn what it's like to handle someone who doesn't know how to take no for an answer," Renée replied with a grin.

After she considered the dangers of what she had planned, Renée had to admit that she enjoyed this topsy-turvy, gender-bending world.

Daniel frowned. "You're enjoying my discomfort way too much."

"Not as much as I would if it were Tony stuck here instead of you."

Osaka laughed at the idea, but then realized one slight problem.

"All well and fine, but where is this brothel that I'm supposed to already know where it is?"

"Good point." Renée returned to Elizabeth. "I know this must sound like a weird request, but could you direct my friend to his, uh, place of business from here?"

The preacher looked at Renée in astonishment. "He doesn't know?" She then piously added, "And from what I've heard you have spent some time there as well."

Of course Renée hadn't considered that possibility. "I need to know the best way to go from the back of the church. Once he gets his bearings, he should be fine." Renée hoped it wouldn't be too hard for Osaka to figure out where it was from there.

For a moment, the preacher woman looked confused. "Have him go right once he leaves here, make a left at the bank, then ride past the saloon on the right, and his house of sin will be straight ahead of him."

"Thank you."

Renée returned to Daniel to give him the directions and her gun. "Then look for where all the boys, wait, girls are hanging around. And don't forget I put a gun to you and made you go along with me, and you have both horses and my gun because you managed to gain my confidence before you shot me dead. They'll probably wait until tomorrow to check out your story, but by then we'll either have them all in the jail, or we'll be dead."

"Or needing a long hot shower to wash off the stain on my soul." Osaka mounted his horse and picked up the reins to Renée's horse.

A few minutes later, he slowly rode out of the shadows next to the bank and onto the small town's main street. As he passed several closed businesses and approached the center of town, he heard loud conversations. "Obviously going in the right direction," he begrudgingly mumbled.

When he reached the next intersection, he could see the saloon where all of the noise spilled out of. Straight ahead as Pastor

Elizabeth had described sat the building where his character called home. Out front stood several horses tied to the hitching bar. He tried to make his way through the shadows thrown up by the light from the saloon, but unfortunately, a woman coming out of the bar recognized him.

"Hey, you were the one who helped Earp escape." Before Osaka could respond, she had her gun out and aimed at him. "Mrs. Barlow is going to be glad to see you."

Based on the speed her gun came out of its holster, Osaka correctly assumed this was one of the gunslingers. "Here we go," he whispered to himself.

"Put your gun away before you do something stupid, cowgirl. Is she with my boys?"

Apparently, he used the correct amount of authority to confuse the gunslinger. "That's right, and I'm taking you to her."

Osaka softened his tone. "I'm surprised you aren't sampling some of my boys. Why don't you let me see what I can do about that?"

This was enough for the gunslinger to holster gun as she walked Daniel's horse to the front of the two-story cathouse. She offered Osaka a hand, which he used to dismount.

As he walked ahead, she gave him a hearty slap across his ass, forcing him forward. It took all of Osaka's resolve to not haul off and coldcock her.

When Osaka entered the door, he found the front room full of half-dressed men chased around by yelling women. Then one of his boys recognized his return. "He's back!" This brought everyone to a standstill while they followed his pointed finger to Daniel. They then rushed to his side and demanded that he explain what had happened.

From behind the gaggle of men came a powerful voice. "Yes Monsieur Mustache, where have you been?" The crowd around Osaka opened up to reveal a taller than usual woman dressed in a black leather blouse and skirt matched against her long black hair and bright blue eyes. Her appearance demanded attention.

Osaka forced himself to lock eyes with the dominate personality. "Oh you know." For dramatic effect, he pulled Renée's gun from his waist and tossed it on the floor in front of her. "I took care of a little business you failed to do."

Barlow reached down, picked up the gun, and examined it. "Earp's gun. How did you manage to relieve her of this?"

"I would love to share my story with you as soon as I have a few drinks and change into something more comfortable. In the meantime, why don't you and your girls enjoy yourselves with drinks on the house until I return?"

Barlow continued to approach Osaka until her face was inches from his. She took the back of her hand and stroked his cheek. "For your sake and the sake of your boys, I certainly hope it's believable." With her eyes still locked on him and a smile of pure evil, Barlow handed the gun back to Osaka and grabbed his crotch. "Or we can have a little fun right now."

It took all of Osaka's self-control not to react. "Come on girls. The most beautiful men west of the Mississippi surround you, and they are waiting to meet your every desire. Drink up!"

A loud yell went up as his boys took their cue from their boss, grabbed Barlow and her girls and led them to the bar.

Osaka took the opportunity to climb the stairs to find his room. It didn't take long to notice the double doors at the end of the hall. He opened it and couldn't believe how well appointed the real Madame Mustache had furnished it. "I could live with this."

He walked over to the closet and after he checked out the contents decided he would look ridiculous in any of the outfits. "Shit. No way around it. Thank god there aren't any cameras to take a picture with me in one of these."

It was then that Osaka noticed something off about the back wall. He pushed the clothes out of the way for a better look, and after he felt around, found a hidden latch. When he pulled on it, a door sprung open to reveal a passageway. "This could come in handy."

He returned to the business at hand. He knew he needed to keep the attention on him, so he bit his lip and picked out the most whorish outfit. He then spent the next horrifying twenty minutes figuring out the sequence required to dress.

When he left to head downstairs, he hesitated at the top of the stairs and took a deep breath. As he walked down the stairs, Osaka exaggerated his movements to accent how he imagined his counterpart would have. A little Mae West with a touch of Marlena Dietrich. Much to his further humiliation, it had the desired effect as the cowgirls in the room took notice with a series of catcalls in his direction.

Osaka sashayed over to the man pouring the drinks, grabbed one, downed it, and motioned for another. He then walked over to the couch Barlow had made herself comfortable on and sat down next to her. "You needn't worry about Earp any longer. I left her dead on the road five miles outside of town."

Barlow wasn't convinced. "Now how could little old you get the drop on one of the stone cold killers of the Western Frontier?"

"The same way I could do the same thing to you or one of your hired guns Mrs. Barlow, by a man's guile." Osaka could feel the bile backing up in his stomach as he motioned the boy with the bottle of whiskey over. "Leave it honey." Osaka scanned the room and pointed out two of the more attractive boys. "Have them come over and entertain Mrs. Barlow. She has much to celebrate tonight."

"Yes Mr. Dumont."

"So not Mustache to my boys, good to know," Osaka thought.

Fortunately, Barlow bought his story and began to loosen up. Over the next three hours, Osaka witnessed things no one should have to remember, but gamely played his role as Barlow and her hands drank and whored their way through the large structure. Though most of the clients had made their way upstairs to the different bedrooms, it wasn't until well after four o'clock the next morning that the two with Barlow finally convinced her to head up. "Take her to my room."

The two hesitated and looked at Osaka. "Just this once. It's a special occasion and I want Mrs. Barlow to remember the night fondly."

Fortunately, he could tell the whiskey had the desired effect, as Barlow stumbled when she tried to rise. Both boys grabbed one of her arms and helped steady her while Osaka pointed to the stairs. "I'll make sure no one disturbs you."

Osaka waited until he heard the double doors close behind them before he scanned the downstairs to see if anyone was still conscious. He then searched for the backdoor to the alley behind the house. He slowly and quietly opened it to peer out. "Renée, you there?" he whispered.

A figure moved out of the shadow of a carriage and walked slowly toward Osaka. "It's me. What took so long?" When Renée came close enough to see Osaka framed in the light, it took all of her self-control when she saw what he wore. "Holy shit. I didn't know they made cowboy outfits in those colors. And the fringes. Now I know where the Village People found their clothing designs. Red and how many shades of blue are there in the world?"

Danile frowned as he handed Renée her gun. "All right already. Can we move on now? Barlow is drunk and upstairs with two of my boys to keep her busy, so we should start with his hired guns."

When he turned to go inside, Renée took a moment to let the last of her giggles out before following. "You do know the real tragedy is I don't have a camera to record this."

"Yeah, yeah."

When they got inside, Osaka threw her a blanket. "The ones left downstairs are shitfaced, but put that over you just in case."

They made their way to the top of the stairs. After a quick discussion, they drew their guns and entered the first two rooms.

Osaka put his finger to his lips when his startled worker sat up in the bed. He motioned for him to get up and stand on the side of the bed as he made his way to the snoring gunslinger. He put the end of his gun on the side of her head. "Make a sound and I'll blow your head off."

One bloodshot eye slowly opened and then got big when she saw him smiling down on her. "Get something to tie her to the bed, and throw me that shirt."

Though confused why his boss wanted him to tie up his client, he complied.

Osaka stuffed the shirt into her mouth, grabbed another to tie around her head, and proceeded to tie her to the four corners of the bed. Osaka found the gunslinger's holster and handed the gun to his prostitute. "If she moves, shoot her."

This brought a smile to his face. Apparently, the gunslinger had roughed him up during their session.

After repeating his actions in two more rooms, Osaka waited by the double doors until Renée emerged from the last room. They nodded in agreement before he slowly turned the knob.

A shock greeted their eyes when they entered the room, and then became humorous as the sight of Barlow's naked body exposed more than her modesty. "She's a he," exclaimed Renée.

In a panic, Barlow sprung across the bed to grab his gun on the nightstand.

"Uhn uh uh," warned Renée. "How about instead of the gun you throw on some clothes so we can talk about how awkward this must be for you."

Osaka addressed his two boys who were servicing Barlow. "I think you can go now, but keep your mouths shut about what you've seen."

Without a word, they grabbed their clothes and left the room.

"I knew there wasn't any way for you to have killed her, though that can be remedied when I call for my girls."

Renée wasn't in any mood for his threats. "Shut up fool. Your hired guns are not going to be of any use to you. We had a plan for how to deal with you, but based on what we witnessed just now, maybe a correction is in order."

Osaka wanted to see how fast they could get out of this gender-bending reality. "Why don't we out him and be done with it. After all, this is 19th Century America."

"What do you think Barlow? Exposure to the town that you are a man or a trip to the territorial judge to stand charges that will see you swinging from the end of a rope?" Renée knew Barlow didn't have a choice.

After giving it some thought, Osaka realized to use Barlow's secret against him would contradict Daniel's personal views on people's rights regardless of how stupid they may be. "Or we can let him leave town quietly with the clothes on his back, and it can remain our little secret."

Barlow took a moment to weigh his options, but in the end, he realized he didn't have any, so he tried negotiation. "What about my land?"

"Sounds like a nice place for us to retire to. On your way out we can stop by the lawyer's office and you can sign it over." Renée figured when she and Daniel left, it would be better for Osaka's namesake to have a nice place to live out the rest of his life rather than end up in an unmarked grave in the California ghost town of Bodie.

Long after Barlow had left in a stagecoach headed for the Mexican border, Renée and Daniel released the gunslingers. Without anyone left to pay for their services, they rode out of town in search of employment.

Renée and Osaka remained holed up in the bordello throughout the day to avoid the unanimous celebrations going on in their name for ridding the town of Barlow's evil.

"Why are we still here?" Daniel asked, as he paced the floor.

Renée looked up from the town newspaper. "I don't know, but

you are driving me crazy. Will you please sit down?"

Osaka took one last look out the front window before he complied. "It's one thing to be tossed from one reality to another like a rag doll, and quite another to add gender reversal to the mix. Though I admit this experience has broadened my perspective on how women manage their limited options. It has made me even more homesick to get back home to Chesapeake Bay and my wife and kids."

Before Renée could respond, the green mist enveloped them.

⬥

Tony and Rebecca found themselves on a dingy street corner under a dim street light.

Rebecca realized they still occupied the same storyline. "Okay, we are still in *The Thin Man* movie, and I am still dressed in clothes I can't breathe or walk in."

"So it appears. Joe Morelli told us we are supposed to bring a name to the kidnappers so they would release some kid. Do you think they are in that foreboding abandoned warehouse?"

Tony watched as one of the doors swung open, and a man in a double-breasted suit with a Fedora on his head walked out. Tony grabbed Rebecca, put his hand over her mouth, and before she could protest, pushed her back into the shadows. "If that isn't a gangster, then my name isn't Nick Charles. Whoever we're supposed to be rescuing is definitely in that building."

"What are we supposed to do about it? You don't have a Tommy gun in any of those oversized pockets of yours, and I doubt I'll be of any use wrapped up tighter than a mummy." Rebecca squirmed back and forth. "I have got to get out of these clothes."

Tony searched the neighborhood and found what he was looking for. "That's where we have to go to find answers, and hopefully we'll find you a change of clothes while we're at it."

Rebecca looked in the direction he pointed. "A bar?"

"No. It's the Lichee nightclub from the *After The Thin Man* movie."

"And?"

"All of my old buddies are there from my days, I mean Nick Charles' days before he married rich you. They'll get us whatever we want, however, be prepared to drink a lot of Martini's and act silly."

Rebecca looked at the out of place club, then back to the gangster smoking a cigarette in front of the warehouse. "Why do either. Why not report the kidnapper's location to the police?"

"Because what we do know about these situations we are put in is that we won't go anywhere until we dance for our puppet masters. At least this little drama has been amusing so far."

"Yeah, that is until one of those thugs shoots us full of holes. Also Tony, you don't have to sound so damn excited about it."

Rebecca started to stutter step her way toward the club. "It feels as if my thighs are wrestling with each other, and I'm going to be the one who loses."

They were almost to the front of the club, when a black 1938 Packard Town car pulled up behind them and a large, pitted face poked out of the front window. "Boss. What's going on? We was to meet up back at the house, and then you disappeared. Oh, hello, Mrs. Charles. I didn't know you was with Mr. Charles."

"That's all right Harold. The Mrs. and I decided we needed to recharge the old batteries before our nightcap."

Rebecca gave Tony a bewildered look.

"Go with it. You're smart, but ditzy. Smart and ditzy remember."

Then Tony addressed Harold. "Stick around. We'll only be a minute."

Harold shook his head and leaned back in the seat. "Yeah, more like you'll be back when the Sun is up." He gunned the motor and drove the car into the parking lot.

Rebecca turned around and marched the best she could into the club. "Fine. Drunk and ditzy it is."

Upon pushing through the curtains behind the open door,

Rebecca was shocked to find the place much bigger than she had expected. Not only that, but against the far wall was a stage set up with music stands for a band.

A small portly man in a tuxedo and thin slicked-back hair rushed to greet the pair. "Mr. and Mrs. Charles it is so nice to see you again. Your usual table is ready for you." He motioned for them to follow.

Tony noticed all eyes turn in their direction as they walked, so he exaggerated his motion to demonstrate he didn't have a care in the world. After the maître d' showed them to their table in front of the stage, Tony grabbed him by the sleeve. "Send over three rounds of martinis for both of us. We have some catching up to do."

"Right away Mr. Charles." He smiled and started to walk away, but Tony stopped him short. "Could you please send someone outside to tell our chauffeur that Mrs. Charles requires him to go to the house to bring her something a little more casual to wear? He can have the maid pick out the clothes."

"Very good Sir."

Tony reached into his pocket and pulled out a wad of cash, selected a fiver, and handed it to him.

"Thank you, Mr. Charles." The man politely bowed and left.

Rebecca leaned in close to Tony. "What are we supposed to do now? Do you recognize any of these people from the movie?" Rebecca continued to squirm in the booth. "It feels as if someone put my boobs in a vise and squeezed them."

"We drink, and we wait."

"I can do that."

The drinks arrived, and after they ordered another three rounds and pounded them down, Tony rolled his head to let it fall on her shoulder. "You look perfectly lovely tonight my dear."

Rebecca shrugged and played her part. "You're only saying that because I'm rich."

"That, and you are truly a vision of beauty."

As the next round of martinis arrived, three swarthy men

approached their table. "Nick Charles and the Mrs. Boys, I told you no marriage to some hotsie totsie bird would change our Charles." Without asking, the three grabbed chairs and sat down at the table.

"Well hello boys." Tony added tongue in cheek, while he twiddled with the olive stick. "Why don't you join us?"

"So what are you here working on Nick? Rumor has it you're looking to help spring that scientist that got snagged."

"Well you got me all wrong boys. I'm retired and living off of this marvelous creature's fortune." Tony leaned forward and lifted Rebecca's hand to his face to kiss.

Rebecca added enough upward resistance to his pull so when he released her hand, she smacked him in the mouth only enough to sting. "You better believe it. All Nick is interested in these days is drinking way past dawn and blowing wads of my fortune down at the track."

The three thugs broke up in laughter, slapping each other on the back. "That's some wife you got there Nick."

"Ain't I." Rebecca then noticed a dangerous looking man approaching their table with his muscle. "Ton…, I mean Nick; trouble is on the way."

Dressed in a black pinstriped suit set off with a matching pork pie hat, the man oozed mob. He stopped short and removed his hat to reveal slicked-back hair as dark as his suit. "Good evening Mrs. Charles. Would you be a dear and let me have some time alone with Nick?"

To Rebecca the tone of his voice signified that he wasn't asking her permission. "Oh no. That's all right. Nicky doesn't need to hide anything from me."

She may not be buying it, but the muscle behind him made it clear the three thugs had to go, to which they unhesitatingly complied. "Well it's been nice to see you and the missus again Nick. We'll catch you later down at the track."

As they departed, the mobster pointed to one of the vacated

seats. "Do you mind?"

"It's a free country; that is if you're buying the next round." As much as Tony could handle his fair share of alcohol, six martinis in rapid fire had taken their toll on him. When he looked at Rebecca, he could tell he wasn't the only one.

To Tony's relief, the mobster ignored his request and got right down to his ugly business. "You were supposed to bring me the name of the person who stole my money. Where is it?"

"That all depends on your part of the bargain."

"Yeah, where's the girl?" Rebecca's alcohol addled mind blurted out.

"You'll get her back alive when I get my money, or you'll get her back to bury the body. It's up to you." To underscore his threat one of his thugs pulled back his coat to reveal his snub-nosed Smith and Wesson 38.

Before Tony could overcome his relief that it was indeed a girl, a medium sized man in his early twenties pushed by the server, which forced the tray he carried to crash to the floor. Before anyone could react, he had his gun out and pointed at the gangster. "I know I promised to let you get Selma for me Mr. Charles, but what kind of a man would I be if I didn't try? Where is she Dancer?"

Based on the way he held the gun, Tony could tell the young man had little training. He could also tell that the gangster's bodyguards knew this as well. "Well look who just came in." Tony pointed toward the front, and as the young gunman's eyes followed, Tony snatched the gun from his hand. "Now, why don't we all pretend this never happened, David. Go home and wait for my call."

One of the bodyguards had other ideas and reached for his gun. "Uhn uh uh, I'll drop you before you can pull it," Tony warned.

Dancer waved him off and snarled at David. "I could care less about a loser like you as long as I get what I want."

Rebecca clapped her hands in delight. "This is great. Don't worry, fella. These movies always have a happy ending. By the way, how much money are we talking about?"

When the waiter spilled the contents of his tray on the floor, all of the club's vibrant activity had abruptly stopped with everyone's eyes intensely glued to the Charles table.

"What the hell." Tony thought. He stood up still holding the gun, and raised his other hand as he exaggerated his drunken state. "I want to thank you all for being in on Mr. Dancer's and our little charade. Now that I have your full attention, comes the best part." Tony looked down at Rebecca who had nodded off with her head on the table. "You know what that is, don't you dear?"

Without lifting her head, Rebecca answered, "A good night's sleep?"

"Probably a good idea, but no. How about a scavenger hunt to find the missing Selma? The best part is whoever finds her gets to pick out one of my lovely wife's hats to keep."

Enraged, Dancer jumped out of his chair, which prompted Tony to point the pistol at him. "All part of the gag folks. Your first clue is they have her holed up in an abandoned warehouse a couple of blocks of here."

The one hundred odd people in the club promptly made a beeline for the door, leaving those at Tony's table alone in the club. At that moment, the band returned to an almost empty room for their next set. They looked around confused.

Tony called out to the band. "How about starting off with Stardust for me boys?"

"I'll kill you and your glitzy wife for this." Dancer's face was bright red with rage.

"Excuse me for a second." Tony reached down to shake the now snoring Rebecca. "Honey, could you retrieve that land deed from your, you know from your..."

Without saying a word and without any regard to propriety, Rebecca rose up just enough to reach into her blouse and pull out the paper. She barely managed to hand it to Tony before she plopped her head on the table and went back to sleep.

Tony waved the land deed like a red towel in front of a bull. "I can't imagine what's so valuable about this plot of land, but knowing plot lines for this time period, my guess is it's either gold or mineral rights."

This was too much for Dancer's men, who went for their pieces, but once again, the luck of Nick and Nora held, as a man in a plain brown suit that screamed flatfoot, came up from behind them. "Your men pull their guns and you'll be advertising for new help, Dancer."

It took a moment to remember the cop's name. "Right on time, as usual Lieutenant Abrams."

Abrams' uniformed officers proceeded to take the guns away from Dancer and his thugs. "So Nick, where's the girl, and who killed the professor? Or is this another one of your crazy stunts that is going to make me look like an idiot, again?"

"I don't know. What do think Dancer? Do you think they found Selma yet?"

"You was supposed to bring me what I wanted so I wouldn't need her anymore. Come on Nick, will you ever do what you says you was going to do?"

A commotion that emanated from outside grew louder until the doors burst open, and a flood of revelers danced into the club. Carried forward in the middle of this mob, one individual looked out of place. "I believe the girl is here, Lieutenant."

Abrams whipped his head around to see Selma approach the table.

With her shaky finger pointed directly at Dancer, she announced, "He's the one who killed my uncle. I saw him do it."

One of the revelers shouted to Tony. "I'm the one who found her Mr. Charles. When do I get my hat?"

Tony then saw Harold with a handful of women's clothes trying to make his way through the crowd. When he finally made it to the table, Tony requested, "Harold, take that guy to my house to pick a hat to take home to his wife."

Hearing this, Harold sighed as he handed Tony the clothes. "Yes Mr. Charles."

After the officers led the criminals away, and Selma exited arm and arm with David, Tony sat down with a look of satisfaction as he waved to his server. "A round for the house on Mrs. Charles, and bring me three more."

The sound of his voice brought Rebecca abruptly upright, her eyes partially open. "You say the nicest things to me."

Tony laughed at her condition as he watched her slowly slip off her chair to disappear under the table. Tony lifted her limp body in his arms. "I guess that's it for us. Check, please."

Tony wore a satisfied smile as he headed to the exit. "I'm going to miss this illusion." For the first time that he could remember, he had enjoyed a completely farcical situation without dragging all of his baggage along for the ride.

Before they could reach the door, to the amazement of those in the club, Nick and Nora disappeared behind a wall of green mist.

The check arrived at the sidewalk café overlooking a beautiful plaza in downtown Havana where Phoenix and Adonis had finished a late breakfast. Phoenix was about to pay for it with the device Franklin gave her when she looked up to see Sean Anthony instead of the server. "This can't be good."

Sean Anthony patted Adonis on the back. "Sorry Adonis, but we have some urgent business to attend to by ourselves."

Before Adonis could object, he found himself alone. "Damn, I wish just once someone would show a brother a little respect."

Phoenix stood next to Sean Anthony on a hill that gave them a panoramic view of San Francisco Bay. "So this is what it's like to stand in the middle of a postcard. This could most definitely be one of the most beautiful places I've ever seen."

Sean Anthony wasn't in any mood to enjoy the scenery. "This is one of Durius' planets. Aaron took Lydia, and we are here to take her back."

Excerpt • Book VI
From the Judgment In Time Series
Judgment of the Gods

Sean Anthony stopped short and looked confused. "I don't think we are alone."

"Aaron again?" Phoenix asked.

"No. Something much more powerful. In fact, something I've only heard rumors about over the years. You ever wonder who someone like Dad answers to?"

Phoenix shrugged. "Once or twice, but we all have been too busy to go metaphysical."

"One thing Mom and Dad agreed on while they raised me, besides to enjoy life, was how best to balance my humanity with the powers I inherited from Dad."

Sean Anthony poured himself some water before he continued. "My days as an evangelist served solely to hone those skills. To tell you the truth, I never looked past Dad for any higher entities."

"Because that is the way I wanted it," a booming voice announced.

CPSIA information can be obtained
at www.ICGtesting.com
Printed in the USA
BVHW031353050319
541836BV00001B/8/P